OUR FRIENDS IN GOOD HOUSES

PRAISE FOR *OUR FRIENDS IN GOOD HOUSES*

'Rahul Pandita's unhurried novel reminds us that a good book is the original "immersive reality." He ventures where only a novel can—inside the mind of a character—to explore what happens when a man longs for mooring. What are we to do when everything worth living for, like love and home, bears the heaviness of permanence, while the only life worth living feels light and nomadic? The novel is addictive ...'

—Manu Joseph

'In [Pandita's] tingling meditation on impermanence, I heard many things, things denied to the ear: nourishment, need, aloneness, the heart's acoustic of spade moving soil, hitting stone.'

—Sumana Roy

OUR FRIENDS IN GOOD HOUSES

a novel

RAHUL PANDITA

FOURTH ESTATE · *New Delhi*

First published in India by Fourth Estate 2025
An imprint of HarperCollins *Publishers*
HarperCollins *Publishers* India, Cyber City,
Building 10-A, Gurugram, Haryana – 122002, India
www.harpercollins.co.in

2 4 6 8 10 9 7 5 3 1

P-ISBN: 978-93-6989-541-0
E-ISBN: 978-93-6989-278-5

Typeset in 11.5/16.2 Sabon LT Std
by HarperCollins *Publishers* India Pvt. Ltd

Printed and bound at
Thomson Press (India) Ltd

MIX
Paper | Supporting responsible forestry
FSC® C010615
FSC www.fsc.org

This book is produced from independently certified FSC® paper
to ensure responsible forest management.

HarperCollins Publishers, Macken House, 39/40 Mayor Street
Upper, Dublin 1, D01 C9W8, Ireland

'… we walked
To where it would have wet our feet
Had it been water.'

—George Oppen, 'The Forms of Love'

PART ONE

NON-GROUND

The summer before he turned forty, he lived in New Haven, on its High Street, in an old apartment building. Its exposed brickwork, when he saw it the first time, reminded him of the gas chimneys in Dachau. In the spring of that year, he had been offered a fellowship at Yale. When he received the email in Delhi, he realized that there was a chance to live in solitude after a long, long time; that, at last, he could find space to think without disruption.

The apartment was close to the repertory theatre. It was on the sixth floor and comprised a large living room, bedroom, kitchen and bathroom. He checked into it well past midnight, after being helped with his two suitcases by the driver who had picked him up from JFK and who, en route, finished eating a big bag of oranges. An administrative staffer of the fellowship programme had kept bread and milk and tea bags on the kitchen slab in anticipation of his arrival. If he looked out of the kitchen window, by whose sill he later kept a pot of African violets, he could see, on the street below, a bicycle locked to a pole. He didn't spot anyone take it for a ride; he did not ask the building manager, but he assumed that some student had left it there and had gone back to his life elsewhere.

The bedroom came with a closet that had extra linen and a giant vacuum cleaner. He used the vacuum cleaner once a week after he had done his washing. There was a big brown couch in the living room, with a TV in front of it. The deluge of pharmaceutical advertisements depressed him, so he never switched it on.

On the other side of his bedroom wall lived a young scholar who suffered from incessant bouts of coughing, over which he continuously played 'Nessun Dorma'. Sometimes, they'd pass each other in the corridor, where the scholar would smile without making eye contact.

Five days a week, after working briefly at his office in Horchow Hall, he'd walk past the repertory theatre, crossing the homeless man sitting on his chair, who always looked straight ahead. At that moment he'd remember an old picture of Meryl Streep, who had performed at the repertory as a student of the school of drama. In it, she was kneeling in front of her partner, John Cazale, in a Shakespearean drama, *Measure for Measure*, which played at the Delacorte Theater in New York's Central Park in 1976.

Two years after that performance, Cazale died of lung cancer.

He'd enter the Book Trader Café, past its racks of used books, and order a coffee, taking the corner table outside, his back towards the small wrought-iron gate. And he would wait for Annie. At exactly fifteen minutes past one, she would walk in, put her arms around his neck and kiss him. The kiss was the reason why he always sat with his back towards the gate; he wanted it to surprise him, as if he were not expecting it at all, as if it were not supposed to happen.

Annie smiling, her eyes half closing in the process—he would take her hand in his and caress it, gazing at her hair that was a million hues of gold.

She was a PhD scholar working on the Holocaust; her parents knew Philip Roth well.

Annie drank coffee from his mug, and they shared a tuna sandwich—her favourite.

Most evenings, they walked around, hand in hand, past the red emergency buttons installed all over the Yale campus. Sometimes, Annie took him to her department, where a Fellini film was always on, and someone passed around slices of pizza. On weekends, they went for dinner to a small Italian restaurant near Papa John's. It was run by two sisters who knew Annie and with whom she spoke in Italian. After the elder sister brought in fresh bread, she'd look at him and say, 'Hey, Neel, go easy on the bread. It will make you fat like me.' Then she'd wink at Annie, making her laugh. It was her ritual, a way of accepting him in her circle.

Sometimes they just stayed in his apartment. While he cooked an Indian meal, Annie hovered around with a bottle of Laphroaig, taking a gulp and passing it to his mouth. Later, he'd lift her in his arms from the couch and take her to bed, over the strains of 'Nessun Dorma'. Afterwards, she'd hold him tightly and say, 'We are one now; we are one!' When Annie got high, she spoke in Yiddish and pretended to be her grandmother—who, when she was Annie's age, had fought the Nazis as a partisan—and that he was her lover and there was a cuckold named 'Fascism' beside them in the room.

'Fuck me, fuck me hard,' she would say, looking sideways at 'Fascism'.

He would watch her getting off the bed the morning after, rushing for her classes, her body so warm that he often suspected she had fever. As she put on her jeans, and then her tan boots, he would look at her and say, 'Leave something behind, I am dying.' She would smile seductively (at this moment, her eyes not quite half closing) and say, 'Die!' From the door, she'd then throw him something of hers—her bra, or her hairband, or a napkin with her lipstick mark. After she was gone, he would keep lying in bed, collecting strands of her hair from the white fitted bedsheet, which he then kept in a muslin cloth.

Most mornings, he wrote for some time and then ran up to the East Rock hill. On his way back, he stopped at the Grove Street Cemetery, next to Hezekiah Augur's grave, and thought of how fast the days were passing. His fellowship was to last only for six months, after which he'd have to leave New Haven (Augur never did!). The thought that he may never be able to see Annie again made him sad. Like that unknown student who had left his bicycle locked to the pole, his life, too, was elsewhere. But Annie—what would he do without Annie?

The German mystic Jakob Böhme had provided him with a word for something he always felt deep inside him. The word was 'Ungrund'. It meant non-ground or an absence of ground, the ontological nothingness of being. For forty years, he had struggled to discover a ground, to come out of the void, to find a home. In Annie, he had found it, though he knew it would soon slip away from him.

Annie, too, he thought, was aware of their impermanency. But they never brought up his impending departure. They talked about their lives, their families. And the more important things, they expressed through raw, physical love. Neel wanted to be like that bicycle, not leaving High

Street ever. He imagined getting buried next to Augur, and Annie would visit him, bringing cigarettes and coffee and Laphroaig, and bread from her Italian friends.

Later, a moment came when things with Annie could become permanent. But he lost that with the display of what he could only describe as a kind of paralysis, a benumbing. It occurred at times when a small gesture from his side could salvage everything. And so, the moment of action would pass; and for him, it never came back.

In New Haven, that year, the paralysis left his entire universe with Annie asunder.

In December, six months after he had met Annie, Neel was gone, walking past the menacing dogs at JFK, who reminded him of Abu Ghraib. He knew then that it was unlikely that he would find a permanent ground; a place somewhere—anywhere—he could call home.

*

Neel always believed that it was the greatest responsibility of men to escape the inevitability of their fate—to break away from the path that others, who had come before, had ordained for them. They had to cleave their own passage, even if it meant the white of bone showed on their elbows.

It had taken him twenty-five years to carve his own path, to move out of the orbit his personal history had put him into. It was this impetus, for a future of his own making, that had made the fellowship at Yale possible.

And then, the time had come to return. He did not resist the return; he knew it had to happen. His life was in India;

it was here, over the last two decades, that he had witnessed things ordinary men only learnt of from the newspapers or remained oblivious to all their lives. It had taken grit and a persistent fight against the whale of fate trying to swallow him and make him stew in its dark belly of ordinariness.

He had gone to places in the countryside that were in the throes of civil war. In one of these, there had been a protracted fight between the state and a ragtag army of rebels who wanted to overthrow the existing order. The rebel leaders said they were doing it for the sake of the indigenous people living there. The state had exploited these people, and now the leaders, who mostly came from cities, had come to fight on their behalf so that they could get justice. It took him time to realize that in a war everyone eventually becomes unjust.

He did not know it then, but it came to him later, that by throwing himself in the middle of such tumultuous events, where death (or life) held no value, he was trying to make sense of the emptiness that the Ungrund had sowed inside him. More than that, he was trying to ward off the feeling that he was doomed to come back to a home that was not his idea of home at all. It was the return to this feeling that he resisted when the time to leave Yale came close, not the idea of return itself.

At that time, he would not have imagined Annie offering him a way out, or that he would not be able to take it and, as a consequence, return first to a home that did not feel like home at all, and then go back to the war zone.

Sitting next to an old man who slept as soon as the flight took off, Neel declined the Indian meals offered by the air hostess, but accepted a bottle of ginger ale. He wanted to open the overhead bin and take out the muslin cloth from his suitcase and touch Annie's hair. But a severe exhaustion had seized him. The plane, with its enormous thrust, had become his purgatory. On the screen in front of him, the Atlantic was an inky, fathomless surface. At some point over the ocean, he fell into a state of semi-sleep. On the screen, then, appeared Annie, a little terse. 'Come back, I want you to eat so much bread that you become fat,' she said. He woke with a hypnic jerk—there was no Annie, and the flight was now approaching Europe. The man next to him snored lightly. Neel ran his eye over the aisle; it was empty. From some seats came the dim light of screens. He stayed awake like this for several hours, his abdomen in knots. Then he fell asleep again.

He was woken up by a little turbulence. His co-passenger was awake now; there were breadcrumbs all over his clothes. Neel noticed that they were now passing over Afghanistan. He'd soon land in Delhi and get sucked into a life that Georges Perec had described as an 'enveloping atmosphere of obligations'.

When the flight landed in Delhi, it was afternoon. In the December smog, there was hardly anything visible. He got down on the tarmac and felt as if he'd be unable to walk. He wobbled in that state to Immigration, and then, near the exit, passed a man, most likely a customs officer, who pretended not to look at anyone in particular.

An hour later, as Neel crossed the toll gate—after which was the satellite town he lived in—a thought took hold of him: a hundred years ago, what would have been in this place where his house now stood? An old British map of the area showed the names of villages that still existed. But everything around had altered. The villages were surrounded by apartment complexes and shopping malls. No matter how many of these shiny galaxies were built, there were always people to fill them up. Amidst such modernity, the old ways kept surfacing, if one paid attention. In the neighbourhood park he sometimes went to, old women from the villages sat in a circle, mumbling songs of longing and of separation from their fathers' homes.

He had returned to live in a house that, in these parts, was referred to as a 'builder's flat'. It meant a certain homogeneity, and more than that, a decay of vision. In these flats, most residents had assimilated their parking spaces (or balconies) with their living spaces, where they kept their St Bernards (in the terrible heat of the Indian plains) and cheap imitations of the Buddha, and where they lied to their bosses on their cell phones.

He lived on the second floor with his father, who wore pyjamas, and shirts Neel had discarded. Father preferred these to the ones Neel would gift him on birthdays. He had nowhere to go, he would often say. It was he who had named Neel after Neel's great-grandfather. It surprised him because Father did not have much regard for Great-grandfather Neelkanth, who, in turn, had been named after the blue-throated god. Having lost his wife while she delivered their son, Neelkanth had spent the rest of his days in a haze of opium, courting several women in his village. But the blue-throated god—whose marriage, when they were in Kashmir, they would celebrate with more fanfare than that of their sons and daughters—still occupied a central place in their lives. Some last-minute wisdom had made Father shorten the name to suit the new world around him—Neel. In his younger days, when Neel erred, as parents often think teenagers do, Father would register his disapproval by remarking that he had turned out to be a vagrant like his great-grandfather. Even after Neel's books were published and went on to win awards, he remained unsure whether Father saw these as achievements, whether he was proud of him for having made something of his life. In any case, these conversations are difficult to have, and perhaps they are futile, too.

As Neel entered his house, he looked at Father and realized how drastically he had aged in the last few years. This had not been evident to him while he was here, while he saw him every day. Back when Neel was young, he believed that Father was so strong that he could brave the wrath of eagles to prise eggs from their nests if his children desired. Father—a village boy, born next to a mighty river, which then tumbled across the Line of Control into the part of Kashmir now under Pakistan's control—was a swimmer, cricketer and (without caring for yoga) the best performer of headstands. As a child, Neel never even saw him catch a cold. He was the man who would sing to his wife, in a burst of romantic Bolshevik sentiment, about his inability to buy her silk saris. She had been affected by events that had unspooled twenty-five years ago, making her lose control over her limbs and her voice. At a time when Neel could afford to buy her silk saris, she could wear nothing but cotton maxi dresses. Neel remembered Father's home in the village, where the roar of the river would lull one to sleep; there was a spring next to it, and exquisite sculptures of gods and goddesses by the boundary wall. It was unlike the home Father would later build in the city—with a kitchen garden and a tap gushing with water.

One day, the home in both the village and the city vanished. What was left was a lifelong spell of anxiety, a result of this loss.

What anxiety would Neel's own loss bring? He dreaded the oncoming of evening, a time when he needed Annie the most. But he'd have to accept that she was far away, and the distance was not only due to the inevitability of geography. So, he'd have to bear the evening alone, and the night, and a lifetime.

Neel unpacked his suitcase, taking out clothes to put them in the washer.

'Are you going to put clothes in the washing machine?' Father asked. 'Do it tomorrow.'

Neel knew there was no point in telling him that they had the biggest water storage tank in the vicinity. He switched on the device that displayed the water levels; it indicated the tank was two-thirds full. But what is the point? He let it go. He could wash the clothes tomorrow.

The shortage of water had been a nightmare.

Their Muslim neighbours in Kashmir, who would send Hindu families like theirs a piece of meat on Eid, had all at once turned against them. They were seized by a sudden bravado—by a fantasy of a separate country, a country where someone named after a Hindu god would not be welcome. In their little Himalayan abode, there was a time when a madman would walk with a leather sack of water, asking the severed heads of the sheep outside butcher shops if they were thirsty. But in 1990, the neighbours refused water to a newly-married friend of Father's, shot outside a mosque while he was returning from office. The man had died begging for water. At that time, the madman would have been the only one with sanity. All those with names drawn from Hindu gods and goddesses, and names that, for example, meant 'the light of the family', had to leave in the darkness of the night.

In exile, in the harsh heat of the Indian plains—long queues for a trickle of water.

The lived nightmare also led to a real, recurrent nightmare—a robber would sneak into the house and would try to strike Father with a hammer he carried in his hand. In his sleep, rendered helpless, Father would produce a sound, as if he were touching a live wire.

A week after Neel was back from America, he came home one night and, as he closed the door after him, heard a sound coming from his parents' bedroom. Rushing there, he found Father sitting on his bed, while Mother, alerted by the same sound, stared mutely at him.

'What happened?' Neel asked.

'Nothing; it's a nightmare.'

A nightmare. Not *the* nightmare. Father never acknowledged its recurrence.

The bile the sound brought to Neel's mouth—some friends believed that Neel ought to swallow it back and never speak of it. These friends, who had taken it upon themselves to issue certificates on what constituted a nightmare, claimed that silence was for the best—for the sake of a larger peace.

They did not realize that for Neel at least, it was impossible to move on by simply feigning forgetfulness.

*

Neel is ten, when a man living in their neighbourhood drops in at their house. He has recently become the sales representative of a pharmaceutical company, and is accompanied by another boy of Neel's age, whom Neel knows as well.

Earlier, Neel had seen the man parade a beautiful electric-blue paper cutter in the shape of a half cookie. It had 'Brufen'—the painkiller his company was promoting—etched across it. Neel desperately wanted it.

That afternoon, the man says that he is offering the two boys some puffed rice. Whoever finishes it first will get a Brufen—he declares this as though he's Julius Caesar. Neel is determined to win it—the blue paper cutter flashes in front of his eyes. The puffed rice is poured into steel bowls; Neel feels he has been given a bit more, but there is no time to raise objections. Both boys begin to gobble big handfuls of puffed rice. Neel finishes first. He is ecstatic. The man looks at him and smiles. 'The winner will now get a Brufen,' he says. Neel extends his hand; the man digs into his pocket and takes out a tablet of Brufen instead of the cutter. He drops it into Neel's eager palm.

Neel feels a storm building inside him, a blizzard that once made his family spend days isolated in a hut up in the mountains. But how he responds to it makes him aware, for the first time, of an inner strength he did not know he possessed.

He laughs hard, and, for a moment, the pharmaceutical salesman is taken aback. He had expected a different response. But that would have given him deeper joy, and with his laughter Neel denies him that.

Many years later, the man comes to Neel's house in Delhi and suggests that they install a washbasin in the living room—for guests to wash their hands after meals, he says. That day, Neel realizes that revenge has had its way. The man has been left far behind, in his ideas, in his vision, in the way he wears sneakers with cheap formal trousers.

Neel does not feel joy; he feels sad for the man.

*

In November, a month before his fellowship comes to an end and he is to fly back to India, Annie appears at his door, her bicycle helmet in her hands. From the way she stands at that moment, Neel becomes aware that she is about to say something vital.

'Will you come home?'

'What do you mean?'

'I mean *home*. Home as in New Jersey, where my parents live.'

What she is proposing is that he accompany her to her parents' house and stay for the Thanksgiving holidays.

He has a flight in two days; he is going to Austin to the Harry Ransom Center, to have a look at David Foster Wallace's papers. The center is shut during holidays, but a friend in the University of Texas knows the director and has promised to make it accessible. Neel can easily postpone the visit and go to Austin once the holidays are over. That Annie is inviting him to her home means something. She is holding him by hand and leading him to a nebula. There will be no void, and the perpetual dread he feels in his heart cannot follow them there.

'I cannot come, Annie. I have to go to Austin.' His own voice surprises him. Annie has stopped looking in his direction.

'Okay,' she says.

*

With Annie, there had been nourishment, there had been succour.

He makes several trips with her to New York. She takes him to the MoMA, and from its store buys him a Rothko print. One weekend, they go to the Morgan Library & Museum, to an exhibition on Hemingway. He wants to copy a line from one of the displayed letters. A Black guard notices his predicament and offers him a pencil stub to write with. Later, in the museum café, he thinks about it. In the guard's mind, he was pursuing something important. Or maybe, the offer to help was simply part of his training.

That evening, they go to the South Street Seaport, where they drink beer in a pub, under a photo of an Italian mafioso, who—Annie whispers in his ear—used to frequent the bar and never paid a penny. They take long walks in Central Park and stop by the lagoon where Holden Caulfield wonders where the ducks have gone.

In the middle of this, while they cross a street or when she keeps her head on his shoulder and drifts off, a strange feeling returns to Neel. It is a premonition in the shape of a ghoul, who whispers in his ears—*this and no further. Try and make things more solid with her, and I will ensure the relationship curdles.* It occurs to Neel that he needs to ignore this ghoul. Annie, too, knows of his paralysis, she knows he needs nudging.

On the night they first made love, Annie had to initiate. She had visited that night; she sat cross-legged on the sofa and tied her hair several times before she was satisfied with it. They had a drink and then ate pasta from the box it came in. Neel had wanted to serve it properly, but Annie rejected the idea.

'I thought Italians were particular about pasta.'

'The only thing Italians are particular about is living,' she said.

They talked, the conversation veering off to an urban legend about Jewish girls at Yale—how they'd do terribly in exams if they passed through one particular gate on campus. They discussed a professor they both loved for her Hegel scholarship and her friendliness. As Neel contemplated whether he ought to hold her, Annie looked at him and said, 'Can you hold me?'

Two minutes later, she was kissing Neel and he kissed her back, and they made love, establishing a pattern for the rest of their time together—from the couch he picked her up, carrying her to bed. He delicately bit her arms, ran his fingers over her nipples, traced her spine, thinking about how much her ancestors must have struggled to keep themselves alive, the result of which was this body that he could hold, trembling slightly with an excess of pleasure.

And now, what does he want? How will this thing work?

He cannot be here any longer. He has to leave for India next month, where his absence, he knows, is making Father jittery. There are things Father cannot handle in the wretched city; he doesn't know the world of ATMs and

OTPs and apps through which cabs and electricians and heart medicines can be called. He could manage these things the old-fashioned way, but even that he finds difficult now. Neel is aware of Father's anxiety about things falling apart in his absence.

What will it be like after his return to India? Will this thing with Annie just become a memory?

Neel imagines visiting New Haven decades later, standing on High Street, outside the café, or by the Italian restaurant. Will he regret not taking the initiative?

*

Neel is about to leave for Austin.

The previous evening, Annie would've taken a train home. He knows she'd have reached late that night.

In general, they hardly speak over the phone. Text messages are exchanged merely to convey something immediate like, 'I am running late by fifteen minutes.'

After a flight to Dallas, Neel takes a connecting flight to Austin. He is in the city by late afternoon. Joshua, who teaches Buddhist philosophy at the university, picks him up; they drive to a café, where Joshua consumes three gimlets and Neel slowly eats a salad. Joshua has immense respect for Neel's people because of their role in propagating Buddhism. But no matter how hard he tries, Neel cannot conjure up an image of his ancestors painting Buddhist murals from Ladakh to Tibet. He wants to tell Joshua that the glory days of his people are over; that they now only write Facebook posts in pidgin English, exaggerating the achievements of their forefathers, while their younger generation worships the IDF because it believes that when Israelis kill civilians in Gaza, the revenge of 1990 has been exacted. As Joshua has another glass of gin, Neel checks his phone—there is no news from Annie.

He sends her a message: 'Hi, I've reached. How is it going?' And then another: 'Sorry I couldn't come. I wish I had. Austin is cloudy; I miss you.'

He doesn't know why, but he feels cloudy inside as well. He keeps his phone back on the table as Joshua goes on about a sale in Macy's and how they should go there and buy a jacket. As Neel nods, his phone vibrates; it's not Annie, but Michael, a staffer from the Ransom Center, asking what time he'll come the next day.

They drive to Joshua's apartment, where he lives with a cat named Proust. They go out again in the evening to a speakeasy, Joshua prevailing upon him to drink an Old Fashioned. Neel keeps checking his phone, but there is no news from Annie. He wants to believe that she is busy with her parents. He wonders what Jewish people do around Thanksgiving. He reminds himself that Annie is not a phone person—she barely checks her device. Maybe she will message later in the night.

He goes to bed early, while Joshua, the practising Buddhist, locks himself in the smallest room of his house, where Neel knows he will chant till midnight. Airports tire out Neel. He cannot imagine what it was like to enter an American airport before 9/11. Now, everything is a nightmare.

The next morning, he is at the center. Michael leaves two cartons of papers for him. He goes through them, making notes with a pencil in a small notebook. In the afternoon, he breaks for lunch and walks to a food truck close to the center, where a Pakistani man offers rice and lamb for five dollars. It makes him long for his mother's cooking. He sits on a bench with his Styrofoam tray and feels the warmth of the afternoon sunshine. He calls Annie, but finds that her phone is off. Her mother is the only person he has seen calling her. Now that she is home, she may have no need for a phone.

Does she not want to hear from him?

She is possibly angry about his blank refusal to come along.

He can catch a flight at once and be with her.

But all his envisioned actions occur either in the future or in hindsight. In the present, he fails to act.

So, he continues to be in Austin.

Two days pass. There is still no news of Annie. Clearly, she is quite angry.

It is okay, Neel tells himself. I will find a way of melting her heart. I will sing an Italian boatman's song to make her smile. I will tell her that I love her, and that I may leave in a bit, but I will find a way of returning and being with her forever. I will ask her not to worry and to pursue her PhD. Maybe we will do long distance for a while; I'll come to see her, and she can visit during the holidays, and we will make it work.

He imagines them in Delhi at Humayun's Tomb, where they sprawl over a mat and have coffee and pastries. He'll play with her hair, and she'll be curious about the swarms of people around them. They will take the metro, and he'll wait for her to see that it is better than the one in New York.

One more day goes like this. Neel sends Annie another message, without any expectation of an answer. He just wants her to know that he is thinking of her and is ready to make amends.

The whole day, he is at the center, sifting through boxes, making notes, taking photos on his iPhone to refer to later. He is far away from the world Father is familiar with. The history of America, the history of Europe, the history of Dachau—so much has happened; so many writers, with their failed affairs, their morning bloodshot eyes, have poured their lives out into notebooks like the one in front of him. So much ink, so much graphite, so much blood and sweat and tears ...

How much writing has taken place because of an abundance of love ... and how much because of an absence of it?

Five days have gone. He has made friends with Proust, who, like the man he is named after, spends a lot of time in bed. When it's time to leave, he takes a flight to New York, from where he decides to take a train to New Haven. It is fall, and the colours are delightful, and he feels this deep love for Annie and wishes that she were with him. He buys a small bottle of wine from the pantry, and sits in the silent car, taking turns reading a book and looking outside.

It is late at night by the time he reaches New Haven. He books an Uber; it is driven by Robert, a driver he had met earlier, a Black man, probably in his sixties, who makes detailed drawings of buildings and shows them to the passengers he likes. He came to the city in the '60s when everything, he says, was burning due to racial tension. Tonight, Robert is unusually quiet.

'I have been thinking, my friend,' he says when Neel nudges him, 'the white man has caused us pain. But some of us have gone down the wrong path, too. And, Jesus Christ, things have really gone to the dogs. So much violence ... you must be getting the mail surely.'

Neel does, but he no longer opens it. By now, he knows the pattern. The mails are about violent acts on campus. That is what the red emergency buttons are for. The spate of violence has only increased over the last few years.

'We must take responsibility for our lives. The police are the police. The KKK mindset is there. But I look at some brothers in my neighbourhood ... and it is like, I don't know what they are going to do with their lives, man,' he says.

It is a big thing he is sharing with Neel, with a man who is not one among them. Earlier, he had told Neel that the Black community had things to say to Obama, but they'd never accept in public that he had barely done anything for them.

It's a tumultuous time. Ferguson has just happened. Trump is delivering his speeches. The walls of the law school in Yale are full of posters carrying the last words uttered by young Black men before being killed by the police. But that night, Robert holds up a mirror to his own people, to show that not everything can be blamed on the other.

Robert drops Neel outside his apartment. The bicycle is there. The elevator is under repair, so he walks up six flights of stairs. He unlocks the door as strains of 'Nessun Dorma' reach him. He takes out an apple and a handful of walnuts from the kitchen. One of Annie's books is on the bedside table. She uses pressed flowers as bookmarks. He brings the flower to his face as if it were her shirt and would smell of her. At this hour, there is a lot of activity in the frat house across the road. Neel thinks of the many scholars who must've stayed in this room and, like him, watched the stream of people outside. One day, it is all vacated. If you are leaving in winter, like he will, they'll ask you to empty the fridge and keep the heating on, so that the pipes do not freeze. What remnant of himself will he leave behind? He could leave the African violets. But they won't survive without care for long. Who knows when the next occupant will arrive.

I should leave them with Annie. I am coming back to her.

The university reopens tomorrow. Annie will be back. Neel will wait for her at the café. She will have to kiss him. And he will kiss her back very hard.

The next morning, he waters the African violets, putting two cubes of sugar in the pot. It is a cold day and he shivers as he walks up to the Italian restaurant. He has never been alone here or with anybody other than Annie. The older sister is outside, her back against a wall. She is smoking and her other hand is in the pocket of her jacket. Neel stands next to her, as if in a huddle. She looks at him, smiles and extends her pack. He takes one and she brings her lighter to its tip. They smoke silently.

'I made tiramisu, take some for your girlfriend,' she says.

'Let me find her first, she is angry with me.'

'Take her flowers then.'

He says bye and walks across the road, next to the parking lot, where he asks the florist to wrap a bunch of white Peruvian lilies in brown paper. He walks to the café and sits outside at his usual spot. He always finds his table empty, which he thinks is a miracle—the miracle of love. The barista waves at him from inside, and Neel sees that he has started preparing coffee for him.

He flips through an old issue of *Granta*. Annie does not come at her usual time. Neel doesn't feel good. A panic sets inside him. He has a foreboding that, like Father, he will have his own nightmare. Cicero says all philosophy is preparation to die. All his love has been nothing more than a grand preparation to resist it. Ultimately, one dies, whether one is prepared for it or not. No philosophical position, no love affair can stall it. With love, though, we ease into death because we know that there will be someone to plant daffodils by our grave. Neel imagines Hezekiah Augur looking greedily at the daffodils Annie lays on his grave, and then turning towards him and saying, 'Howdy, neighbour?'

He leaves the coffee and sprints towards Annie's apartment. The red buttons—they are like clown noses, mocking him. One of Annie's friends is at the main door; she is rushing out with a pile of books.

'Hey, how is she now?' she almost shouts, as if speaking over some invisible din.

His face turns hot like the plate of an iron. There is a word that occurs to him and keeps flashing through his mind—cauterization.

He does not ask Annie's friend anything. He sprints towards Annie's department, by which time he has reached a point where he can ask.

After his refusal to accompany her home, Annie decided to walk to the station to catch a train to New Jersey. Near a construction site close to the station, she was mugged by an assailant. He also tried to molest her, dragging her along the sidewalk. He took her handbag, in which Neel knows she kept a poem she had written on a piece of blotting paper when she was ten.

At this point, he begins to see things clearly. Annie, it dawns upon him, will always imagine an alternate scenario in which he has agreed to come home with her. Had that happened, this incident would have never occurred. His one decision, his inexplicable dithering, has altered the course of their lives. Which way is he now to direct their future?

After the attack, Annie had been hospitalized with severe bruises, and was later taken home by her parents.

Neel suddenly remembers a distant cousin of hers who is a post-doctoral fellow in the department of Jewish studies. She does not have Annie's address, but knows another student who sent Annie research papers by post a while ago and may have it.

He gets into the train to Newark. He wonders how Annie will react when she sees him. He can no longer look at the colours of fall. He feels drained. Two stops away from Penn Station, his phone vibrates and he finds Annie's text: 'I believe you've been looking for my address. Please do not come here. I am not sure if I will return. You should go home.'

Home. This throws him off. She knows how he feels about the word. She thinks he can go home by leaving her.

Annie is one stop away. But Neel is unable to act now. Paralysis strikes him like a flash of lightning. He picks up his duffel bag and gets off the train. He takes a train going the other way, and in an hour or so, he is in New York, in a dingy pub.

Life is a burlesque dance. His head throbs with pain. In an alternate universe, he's in Annie's home right now, walking past the menorahs and the sepia-tinted picture of the partisan grandmother. They arrange themselves in the lawn outside with wine and bread. Her father says of Roth, with a grin, 'He is a devil!' Her mother puts more food on his plate, saying, you have hardly eaten anything. A late-night cigarette with Annie and then a hurried kiss.

But now it does not matter.

If he once had a river inside him, it has frozen.

As he exits and steps outside onto a street he does not recognize, the ghoul is back, grinning, high-fiving his fellow ghouls.

In December, as his fourteen-hour flight to Delhi takes off from JFK, Neel remembers that he has left the African violets by the sill.

They will die and Cicero cannot prepare him for it.

*

Annie repeatedly shows up in his dreams after he returns to India. In one that's recurrent (recurrent like Father's, he cannot help but notice), Neel finds her staring at his apartment on High Street. She is holding her helmet in her hands as soft flakes of snow land on her golden hair. He calls out to her from his window, but she cannot hear him. He has this longing to hear her voice. 'At least ask me to eat bread that will make me fat,' he tells her. But she keeps mum and only stares at him.

That winter, it snows heavily in New Haven. Robert sends him a video of the apartment. The bicycle's tyres are buried in snow. He wonders where Annie is in that desolation and whether her body still retains a feverish heat.

And: does she still imagine 'Fascism' kneeling beside her?

*

His destiny is small, decrepit hotels in the hinterland, where the meagre staff is already drunk at breakfast, and where strange noises come from other rooms, and the mattress is so stained that it could have come from an abattoir. He is constantly in transit, entering and exiting violent places. He never gives a true picture to Father of what he sees. But sometimes, when his travels become so frequent that he simply leaves one bag at home and picks up another that is already packed, Father says that his journeys are an affliction. He uses an expression in their mother tongue for it—'paed raah'. Feet destined to always hit the road.

It is early January. To escape Annie's memory, Neel takes up an assignment far away from the bedazzling corporate offices of Delhi, in a place where people still don't have enough to eat. The rebels have taken a district collector hostage. His phone begins to ring as soon as the news breaks out. There are television channels that want him to speak about the turn of events. Some newspaper editors want him to go to the conflict zone, so they can publish dispatches from there. He agrees to travel for a newspaper he had once worked with.

That's how he finds himself at the Delhi airport, walking down a carpet with patterns reminiscent of the Soviet era. He takes a flight to the airport nearest to the area of conflict. From here, he knows, he will be in a constant flux. He will have to endure a gruelling seven-hour drive, mostly along a stony road, with thick thorny bushes either side. Beyond this road are the Eastern Ghats, with coffee plantations and a contiguous forest area where he had once witnessed a man getting scalped by a sloth bear.

As the jeep rattles over stones, its chassis sometimes getting scraped by the bushes, his back begins to hurt. He shuts his eyes and thinks of the lemonade his mother used to pour out for him in a tall glass as soon as he'd be back from school.

It is early evening by the time he reaches the small town. He has to go across the river which has no bridge. The collector has been abducted from the 'cut-off area'—a cluster of villages isolated from the mainland after a dam was built over the river. From the town where he has to spend the night, it will take him about an hour to reach the cut-off area. There are no hotels here. His only hope is to secure a room in the circuit house. It is at one end of town, in front of a huge ground strewn with kitchen waste. The caretaker, who loathes making even minimal arrangements for someone who is not a government servant, resists offering him a room, but relents as soon as Neel slips some money into his shirt pocket.

The room, he can see, was once painted a garish blue, but most of it has chipped off, and what remains now is mostly an enclosure of damp walls reeking strongly of mould. The mattress is still in its plastic cover, on top of which there is a cheap bedsheet that has most likely never been washed. He puts his bag in a corner and lies down on the bed for a few minutes. His body still feels in motion. It also feels feverish because of the Mefloquine he had popped before he left. From his bag, he takes out a bottle of a South African insect repellent called Tabard and sprays it all over his body. It will irritate his skin, but it will also offer him considerable protection from malaria. He lies down again, but five minutes later, he grunts and gets up. He needs to figure out a place to eat, and also find an internet kiosk from where he can send his story—there is no mobile network in the area.

The collector would go to the cut-off area every month to monitor the progress of new government schemes. The previous day, he had gone there early with a group of officials. As he stood outside a small hut, talking to a widow about her pension, a group of rebels appeared on bikes. They fired a few warning shots in the air, after which they whisked the collector off on a bike, seating him between two rebels.

Neel finds a small shop that sells groceries; it also has a computer that offers internet access for two hours in the evening. He pays the owner of the facility some money in advance as an incentive to open up daily for a few days. The advance is no guarantee, but at least it will make him feel guilty if he ghosts Neel. For meals, he discovers a shop that sells puffed rice, topped with a boiled potato and a handful of vegetable fritters, served on leaf plates. He eats this quickly, watching a cluster of mosquitoes droning over the shopkeeper's Petromax lamp. He returns to his room and takes a Paracetamol for body ache. Outside, dogs bark relentlessly, and the caretaker, pissed drunk, speaks to invisible ghosts.

The next morning, Neel is at the riverbank, from where he has to take a motorboat to reach the cut-off area. He knows what he has to do once he crosses; he has to look for a man whose heart is brimming with things to say—a heart that Neel will then tip over gently. This requires immense patience, but he is prepared. The motorboat arrives, he gets into it, and in ten minutes, he is on the other side. As he walks towards the first village, his combat shoes getting smeared with mud, he spots a man under a thatched roof sitting on a wooden bench. He reminds Neel of the homeless man outside the repertory theatre at Yale. Like him—Neel can see as he comes closer—the man's face displays no emotion. As Neel enters what looks like a waiting area, the man watches him, then fixes his gaze back on the river in front. Neel walks gingerly and sits on the bench, maintaining some distance from the man. Establishing a precise equation with him is like constructing a delicate wall around a heritage building. The master mason must lay one brick after another. Similarly, through a pile-up of gestures and actions, Neel must build a rapport with this man. Sitting there, he, too, fixes his gaze on the river, and stays like that for what seems like a quarter of an hour. Then, he takes out his pack of cigarettes and lights one. As if it's an afterthought, he looks at the man and offers him a cigarette. The man looks back at him and then at the pack, and quietly takes one. Neel lights it for him. The two men take deep puffs, still not exchanging a word. He shows no hurry, no intention of seeking answers. They are like co-travellers now, taking a little rest during an arduous pilgrimage. Neel has to prove to the man that he is not a police informant or anyone else whose presence will cause him harm. That is the first step.

Long ago, Neel had learnt a valuable lesson from a rebel leader. After he had finished interviewing him, the leader had looked at him and said, 'There is one thing that I liked about you. During the entire interview, your eyes did not hover around; they remained fixed on me.'

'What did that tell you?'

'It told me that your heart is at rest.'

With the same restfulness of heart, by that riverbank, Neel starts a conversation with the man. He tells him that he is a journalist, that he has come to see how people live in these parts and what their daily struggles are.

The man opens up slowly, as if following the steps of some ancient ritual. His name is Lakshman, he says, and he runs a small shop where he sells groceries, or at least tries to. But he is always incurring losses. People buy things from him and say they will pay next month. But their life is hard and the money does not always come. So, they are unable to pay. 'Unlike the businessman from the city, I cannot go to their home and beat them up,' he says. When his wife berates him for being taken in by people, he comes to the river for some time. 'I sit here and tell myself that the universe is much bigger than my life in this village,' he says.

Neel offers him one more cigarette. 'Do you know a place where we can have tea?' he asks.

'There is a shop, but it is closed right now.' The owner has run away because the police are looking for him, he says. 'A big official of the government was taken away from here.' The police suspect the tea shop owner of being in cahoots with the rebels. 'What is one to do?' he asks. 'The big brothers come to my shop, too. They take rice, and sometimes sugar, but they always pay. Beyond that they do not trouble me,' he says of the rebels.

Minutes later, Neel is riding pillion on his motorbike. He drives fast down a narrow mud trail. It looks like the dried-up path of a tributary. A little ahead, they pass a man lying face down under a stunted tree. 'He drinks too much,' Lakshman says.

The bike stops outside a small hut. It is from here that the collector was abducted, Lakshman says. Upon seeing them, a few villagers come out. They surround the bike. They have all seen the collector's abduction. Normally, they aren't likely to open up before a stranger. But this stranger comes with a man they all know. So, they speak freely.

Neel visits every day, leaving the circuit house as early as possible, partially to save time and partially to avoid coming across the caretaker whose cirrhosis he can diagnose from his red, dried-up skin. He files his report every day, and miraculously, the owner of the internet shop keeps his promise.

Five days later, Lakshman asks him not to leave at his usual time. That evening, the rebels hold a public meeting in a village not far from where the collector was abducted and release him. It's a spectacle, a ruse that they have to maintain—of taking into account the will of the people while dispensing 'justice'. The decision had already been taken and it is only conveyed in the presence of the people, who, in any case, understand little. The abduction has kept them in the news, and, also, some leaders have been freed under a secret pact with the government. As soon as the rebels disappear, the villagers garland the collector, and he is taken on a bike towards the river, from where he will catch the motorboat.

Neel takes the same motorboat. He can now send the final dispatch as he had been the lone journalist to witness the spectacle. With that, the assignment is over.

The eatery has shut shop. Neel returns to the circuit house. The caretaker is nowhere. He takes out two biscuits from his rucksack, drinks water from his flask and lies down on the bed. He is tired and falls asleep with his clothes and shoes on.

He wakes up with the caretaker peering over him, as if to check if he's dead. He is startled when Neel moves. He is saying something that Neel does not understand. He gets up, takes a quick shower and is out. He will now make the same seven-hour journey through the forest to the airport. But first, he has one thing left to do. It is an unwritten code, the last act in the series of things he has done to tell a story. He takes the motorboat back to the cut-off area. A little before the riverbank, the motor goes off and the boat ambles towards the bank. Under the thatched roof, he can see a man and he knows that it is Lakshman. He sits next to him just like he had a week ago.

'Have you sent it?' Lakshman asks, using the colloquial 'samachar' for news.

'Yes.'

'Are they happy?'

'The universe is much bigger than their happiness.'

He smiles. Neel offers him a cigarette, which he takes. Come with me, Lakshman says.

Neel follows him on the same mud trail he has taken every day over the last five days. At one point, Lakshman turns left, and then, after about a hundred metres or so, he stops outside a hut. 'Come,' he says. On the mud façade, there is beautiful art created with limestone. Under a small tree in the courtyard, around which Lakshman has tried to grow flowers and vegetables, there's a plastic chair and he wipes it with his gamcha. He gestures to Neel to sit on it. Then he climbs the tree, and from a branch just above Neel's head, he brings down a narrow vessel made of dried bottle gourd. He gets down and sits on his haunches next to Neel's chair. He pours out the local brew into two leaf cups and offers one to Neel. Neel takes it and then, pushing the chair a little away, joins his friend on the floor and sits just like him. It's 9 a.m., and Neel smiles. It's too early for a drink, but he cannot refuse this gesture of friendship. That won't be the honourable thing to do. There is nothing to say. Neel will return to Delhi and there is very little chance that they will meet again. But whenever he has a drink in the city, he will remember Lakshman. He gets up. He shakes hands with him. 'Thank you and take care of yourself.' As Neel gets on the motorboat, he looks at Lakshman, who waves at him and then begins to walk towards the thatched roof structure.

Six hours later, as he nears the city from where he has to take the flight, Neel's phone signal returns. That morning, there had been a big operation by the government forces in the neighbouring state. Several rebel guerrillas and their leaders are dead. The network is weak and he waits to access the photos of their corpses.

His heart is not at rest.

The flight is delayed due to bad weather and it lands in Delhi only at night. He unlocks the main door as quietly as possible, but Father is already standing at the door of his bedroom.

'Have you eaten?' he asks. That is Father, Neel thinks, trying to be Father, Mother and Wife, all in one.

He ignores his question and hugs him, then enters their room. He bends down over Mother and kisses her. Even in semi-darkness, he can see her eyes twinkling at the sight of him. She'd have forced him to eat.

He takes a long shower, washing off the dirt and grime of the assignment, and the residue of Tabard, and drinks a glass of warm milk. Mother believed that a glass of warm milk could cure everything. He checks the internet again for some news, but there is no major update on the encounter.

He wakes up to an extremely cold morning. The city is engulfed in thick fog. The air is so bad that his throat feels scratchy and he can almost taste the acridity. He gets ready quickly and leaves after having two coffees and a breakfast of toast and eggs.

From the window of the metro, Delhi looks like a city witnessing an apocalypse. As the train moves slowly on an elevated platform, he can see on the road below, wherever the fog permits, men huddled around little fires they have built out of trashed cardboard. He takes out, from the inside of his jacket, the newspaper that carries his last dispatch from the cut-off area.

Halfway through, even as his eyes run over the news report, he sees a boy and a girl, who look like college students, get into the train. The girl whispers something in the boy's ears and he looks at Neel. Suddenly, the girl approaches him with her hand on her belly.

'I have pain in my stomach. Can I have your seat?'

He looks up and can see that she wants to trick him, in order to impress her boyfriend. In his head, he is still by that riverbank, walking towards Lakshman.

'In that case, you must get down at the next stop. There is a hospital right there. It could be appendicitis, you know.'

The girl's face falls. She drags herself back to her boyfriend and says something. Neel goes back to the newspaper. The two keep standing, listening to some music through shared earplugs.

After an hour, he is at the other end of Delhi. This is as far as the metro goes. It is a Delhi that not many in his circle have ever been to—it's where the city's poorest live. No Uber comes here, no food delivery apps work. There are no roads, and after it rains, the lanes overflow with sewage. No man or woman from here has ever visited India Gate for late-night ice cream. They do not throng Connaught Place on New Year's Eve. From the metro station, he takes a cycle rickshaw that drops him outside a slum. It is here that men who work as ragpickers or security guards live, while their wives remain employed as domestic servants in middle-class homes in nearby colonies. Early in the morning, these men come out on their ramshackle bicycles, with no lights or reflectors, to work long, gruelling shifts.

Neel walks slowly, and with a look on his face that portrays a deep familiarity with the place. It says: I am not an outsider. At some point, through a maze of brick settlements with asbestos roofs, past water tanks and second-hand coolers and dish antennae, he finally reaches his destination. He knocks once. He waits. For a minute, nothing happens. He does not knock again. He knows the drill. After a minute, a man comes out.

'Hello, Jassi.'

Jassi looks around and then lets him in.

'Will you have tea? I was about to make some,' he says.

Neel nods.

'You have left your phone behind, no?'

'Yes.'

Jassi turns back. It's a small room. On one table, there is a tiny gas stove on which Jassi prepares tea. On the other side, his clothes hang, held in place with a few pegs. There are some books on a table whose broken leg is supported by a pile of bricks.

'How is Gurupriya?'

Jassi looks at him but does not answer immediately. He drops some ginger into the boiling water and waits by the pan whose handle, Neel sees, is broken.

'There is too much activity in Gurupriya's area,' he finally says. 'We have been waiting for a biscuit.' Then, he adds, as he hands Neel the tea, 'I am leaving this place in a few days.'

'Where will you go?'

'It is better that you don't know.'

The tea is done.

'How will I know if Gurupriya is fine?'

'We are all here on borrowed time,' he says. But he makes amends quickly when he notices that Neel is disconcerted. 'Wait for the biscuit.'

Neel gets out and takes the metro. He is too tired to make a stop and meet friends who, he knows, will be having a drink at the Press Club. He returns home. On the pavement outside, the sapling he had planted years ago is a fully-grown amaltas tree. He runs his hand over its trunk. It is barren in January, but a few months later, it will be in full bloom.

'Let us wait for the biscuit,' he whispers.

*

Before going to Yale, he had been living in the builder's flat for six years.

When Adaa saw it for the first time, a month before they shifted into it, she said, 'Oh, I had a different impression of it.' By which she meant, she was expecting a certain fanciness that was evidently missing.

On New Year's Eve, they had gone to a party at her friend's house. It was in an old, posh neighbourhood of South Delhi, where all the houses had the same kinds of cupboards for crockery, and where fights over parking were now a way of life. The friend, Adaa's colleague in film-making, was dancing with others. Adaa joined him. In the meantime, on that foggy, cold night, the colleague's girlfriend emerged out of her bath in a short dress, and stood next to Neel, near a bonfire. Her whole body seemed to exude superiority—as if she saw herself as Cleopatra; as if she had emerged after a bath in donkey milk. They largely ignored one another. He felt out of place, but stayed back as Adaa was having a good time. These were not her people either, but she did not want to believe it.

Adaa always expressed outrage when he mentioned the names of things in Hindi in front of her friends—the names of things like 'spectacles' and 'office'. It hurt her convent-school sensibilities. It took her months to make peace with this habit of his. He wanted to tell her that the sophistication of her friends was limited to terming food as 'grub'. That this was not his life. He lived in quest of other things, for a punctum he felt unable to point to if someone asked.

Back then, he often saw Adaa standing at one end of the living room, a cup of tea in her hand, trying to visualize all that could be done to the space, so it resembled the living rooms of her friends. They ended up buying furniture well beyond their budget. She retained a set of figurines from one of her big brand shoots. They got flowerpots, which they carried in her car, and he watched as she drove, cutting sharply, taking phone calls on the road.

Adaa's college friend had given her a CD that contained a short video titled *Farmer's Breakfast*. It was steamy, a 'story' about a farmer somewhere in the West, who left home to till his fields, but returned after a few minutes, announcing to his wife that he had forgotten to have his breakfast. He'd then hold her and take her from behind. Adaa developed a liking for the video. In her weak moments, she would ask Neel to enact it, especially after having a rough day at office.

In the spring of the following year, it occurred to him that Adaa and he were somehow inching towards a plateau of happiness; that they would be able to bury the bitterness that kept rearing its head between them. There was no tangible foundation for this bitterness; maybe it sprang from the fact that things just did not become whole in their association. Neel kept on feeling out of place and Adaa resented it. She suspected that he had found a home elsewhere. He had not, but he could not communicate this to her.

That year, they got three tree saplings and planted them along the pavement below the flat. Sometimes, after dinner, Adaa would go down to take a short walk with two neighbours she had become friends with. Afterwards, Neel would hear her laughing loudly.

From the balcony, where he often stood, he could see a high-rise apartment. He'd wonder about the lives of the people there. He could spot the silhouette of a couple in one of the flats. Neel imagined things about them. He imagined corner bars and terracotta ashtrays and weekends binging on sleep and *Casablanca*. He imagined a permanency of things.

Spring is a heady time. It is when silk cotton trees are filled with clusters of red flowers, and people put fresh coats of paint on their walls and take short walks after dinner, and young couples eat from the same cup of ice cream and make plans of opening joint bank accounts. Spring passed, and fall, and suddenly, he could no longer see the couple. He had imagined two people in love, listening to Dooley Wilson's 'It Had to be You' over and over again, their home filled with Sunday magazines, and empty teacups, and decanters with lemon-infused water, and table calendars with red circles over extended weekends. A whiteness of vision. They had moved, or were no longer together, or had, to put it in the Mad Hatter's words, lost their muchness.

Is happiness possible? And what is it, anyway?

One day, he took the car out, despite not knowing how to drive well. He went to the neighbourhood park, where he would go running every morning. As he returned, he drove to the parking spot, but veered off a little, crushing one of the saplings. He told Adaa what had happened, and she came down with a gauze cloth and tried to bandage the split.

Neel could feel a future pain. He somehow knew then that things would not be the same; that their relationship would change irrevocably.

And it did.

Things, inexplicable things, kept breaking between them.

Farmer's Breakfast was a thing of the past.

And one day, Adaa left.

Once she was gone, he stopped paying heed to things at home. The sofa became stained, the television remained switched off. One day, he spotted a spider's web on the figurine. Her side of the bed remained vacant and then got covered with books.

Neel remembers one day in particular—it is a month before Adaa leaves. He is about to embark on a long journey. The perilous trip will take him to the heart of the country. His things are packed in a rucksack—a change of clothes, a small bag of medicines, packets of ORS and chlorine tablets, a camera, a voice recorder and a sleeping bag.

Neel cannot convey to Adaa that he has to leave the next day. The air between them is crinkling; no conversation is possible. He is not sure if he will come back; anything can happen in a conflict zone.

At night, when everyone has gone to bed, he sits in the balcony, on its cool tiled floor, and lights a cigarette. It is a period of transition, he realizes later. He is still young, but this time will go away fast. In photographs—he'll study them years later—in the jungle with rebel guerrillas, there's no grey in his hair. But there will come a day when he will feel old and will dwell on the idea of mortality, and the thought will not leave him.

He returns after three weeks, catching the last flight from a city closest to the guerrilla zone. By the time he reaches home, it is midnight. He takes a long shower to clean all traces of the journey, changes into clean clothes and steps out into the balcony. I am back, he says to himself. The city sleeps around him. Adaa is in the bedroom; he has taken the guest room.

What is home? What are its, say, top five parameters? What kind of magic does a space require to convey to a man that it is what he has been looking for all his life? How does communication break? When you say you love someone, what exactly does it mean?

And: how do you unlove a person?

A few weeks before Neel has to leave for Yale, he is at a book launch where he meets one of Adaa's former colleagues. He knows that Adaa and Neel are no longer together. She has been gone for four years, and this is the first time that Neel has spotted the man. He is a copywriter, and in their few meetings in the past, they have simply talked about things of common interest.

'Are you still on the same number?' he asks.

Neel nods, though both of them know he will never call. This is just a thing, one of the artificialities the city revels in.

'Neel.' He calls out his name after they have passed each other.

Neel stops and turns to see the man walking towards him.

'Do you remember that party?'

Neel has seen him at several—they have only met at such gatherings—but he knows instinctively which one he is referring to.

'Do you remember Kabir's girlfriend?'

She is the Cleopatra who stood next to him on New Year's Eve.

'Fifteen days ago, she jumped from the seventeenth floor of this hotel.'

*

Neel wonders if there is anything that moves Father. He has no opinion, except about those who cannot take quick decisions (he abhors tardiness). But apart from such pragmatic pronouncements, he is a man who likes to be home—he never has had any life outside it. After Mother's taking to bed, this has only got exacerbated. There are family marriages in different cities, now that the younger generation is scattered across. He can easily attend some of these to get a break. Neel's sister really tries. She tells him that he can go with Neel, while she will look after Mother. 'You think I am not capable of taking care of her?' she asks, exasperated. Father doesn't say anything; he just smiles. Neel does not press; he understands. Father loves the woman he fell for in college. They have spent almost fifty years together. Her condition is fluid, she can go anytime.

He wants to be around when that happens. Neel does not say this to his sister.

There is not much that Father asks of Neel—neither of his company nor of his time. Not even for something normal, like going out for a meal. It used to make Neel angry, but now this only scares him. Scares him because while the transition is yet not complete, he may be like Father more than he thinks or is willing to admit. He is certainly more like Father than he was, say, ten years ago.

What strange thing constricts Father? He reads newspapers, watches the circus of news on television as it teeters towards a dangerous cliff. He never speaks about Kashmir or remembers it, except at some odd moment when a memory comes to the fore. He has never expressed a desire to return for a visit like most have. He has never shown any sentiment towards the house he had built with such hardship and which he had to leave in the middle of one January night. He never mentions Adaa after she leaves. Not even a 'How is she?' or 'What has she done with her life?' or 'Are you in touch?' Nothing. Neel thinks it's some sort of coping mechanism and, who knows, he may be on his way to acquiring this, too—this strange ability to not think of loss. Or maybe he has an even better coping mechanism than Father's—of preventing loss even before it occurs.

But what does he then do with all this love in his heart?

Maybe he should surrender it to the ghoul, who recycles it into a meal for a million wolves.

Neel has never told anyone, but even in the house his parents had built so lovingly, he had never felt at home. He felt an ontological dissatisfaction, which, when he was a young boy, with scant understanding, he attributed to boredom. It is only years later, when a man—a professor he looked up to—handed over a book to him, thinking that it would help him write the piece he was supposed to (on the condition of exile), that he could pin down his sense of unbelongingness. Neel opened it and came across Ungrund. He knew at that exact moment that there was finally something that explained his predicament.

In that room for visiting scholars, where the professor came and gave him the book, he remembered closing the door and running his finger across the lines. He felt a definitive lightness, as if he had found the answer to a complex mathematical equation.

From here, it became easy.

But what is this ontological dissatisfaction? He does not discuss it with anyone, but even to himself, Neel finds it cumbersome to provide an account, a logos, of this dissatisfaction. He does not know precisely what caused it. There is one incident, though, that he identifies as the moment when he felt most at home. This, then, has become a marker of knowing when he is not; and he is not, for the most part.

The incident is rooted in time past, in their house in Kashmir. It is late afternoon. There is nobody around—both his parents are at work. Neel is sitting in the verandah, when he suddenly feels an urge to hide himself. He looks around and sees a circular bed of roses. In the centre of it is a patch of grass, and he goes there and lies down. He is now hidden from the world; one will really have to come close to the shrubs and peek inside, to spot him there. It is sunny, and in the gentle breeze of the Himalayas, the row of poplar trees sways gently. He closes his eyes and feels the interplay of light and shadow. A crow is cawing in the gentlest way—it is like a lullaby. Neel feels that the universe has revealed itself to him; that everything is in order, and nothing will ever change. It's like a shaman has taken him under his wing and offered him ayahuasca in that circle of love; as though he has crossed a barrier of perception, and now, this sluice gate will never close.

He is naïve. Things do change. The sensation of homecoming just lasts a moment. The sun is shadowed over, the crow flies away, the breeze shifts, and outside, he hears the main gate open. The equilibrium is disrupted. The meditative nature of the universe shifts; it churns. But, in his inner universe, that moment stays. From then on, he tries in vain to stretch the moment to a lifetime.

Much later, Neel comes across a diagnosis for this disposition. Leibniz had considered living in a garden of paradise as one of the singularities of life—in other words, a distinct moment that could not be duplicated. But he also cautioned that such a garden was incompatible with the world in which Adam sinned.

So, this is what has been his search—a yearning for a space that will become his paradise. Neel has craved for it so much that Leibniz's warning does not dissuade him. In every room, every apartment, he has tried to create a patch of grass, a heaven that has eluded him.

The exile jeopardized whatever little permanency of things he had felt. Father's home was not his idea of home, but at least there was space, there was that rose bed. In exile, the roses burn in his eyes; they are set aflame by the scorching summer heat of the first year in the Indian plains. Space shrinks. There are no gardens or apple trees or wooden stairs or rooms (in the plural) or attics. There is only one room, and everything must fit there. What it cannot accommodate is the moment he yearns for, the home he yearns for.

The perpetual search for home manifests itself in a different way in his later years. In Delhi, he comes across home décor magazines, and these make that moment of childhood come alive again. The magazines have no grassy patches specifically matching his vision, but they have beautiful pictures of houses. They are of all kinds, across a range of geographical spaces—in the north, in the south, in hill stations or near beaches. Some of them are not to his taste, but some, he feels, come close to the aesthetic he is after. There is no pattern to what comes close; at least, he cannot sense a pattern. But, in general, he likes rooms that offer space where he can hide; where, as with that grassy patch, things, visible and invisible, are in consonance. In time, other patterns became clear—he dislikes kitsch and gaudiness. He likes an earthy feeling, wood more than glass, windows and balconies opening out into greens—not manicured lawns but those running wild. He likes the frames of exhibition posters, stone busts, handmade kilims, coffee percolators, corners where he can sit on the floor, bedrooms that are sparse, kitchens that have larders and where there is a place to wait close to the stove.

The magazines are expensive, so Neel finds a way to procure second-hand copies from Ashraf, an elderly bookseller who sets up his stall every Sunday in Old Delhi. Each month, he offers a new pile to Neel. Neel sits at leisure, leaving everything aside, away from all distractions, and he leafs through them, spending hours gazing at what feels like home, and quickly dismissing what does not at first glance. It all comes very instinctively to him, like some memory of a former birth.

When Adaa was still with him, she'd get such magazines from her office, where they were available in abundance. When she left, that supply stopped. But there's Ashraf; the magazines keep coming steadily. At times, when Neel does not even feel like it, Ashraf's phone call, the measured excitement in his voice, prompts him to glance at the houses.

Year after year, even after Adaa, Neel lives his idea of home through these pages. In many ways, he is unyielding, firm. But when it comes to home, he is still a nomad; he is a wanderer who has no stars to guide him.

Only during travel—dangerous travel—does the malady called homelessness go away.

In America, once, Neel bought a copy of the *New York Times* from Penn Station. In the Amtrak, while flipping through its pages, he read in one of its popular sections about the marriage of Ved Mehta's daughter, Sage, with a Jewish writer in New York. There was a photo of their wedding day, with a rabbi blessing them. The reporter—after describing how they had lived together in a tiny studio in the Lower East Side—mentioned a 'long desk with a glass top', where they wrote together by day; by night, it became a dinner table, where they ate with friends and had conversations. Neel felt that his idea of home had achieved a poignancy through the mention of this table. As he got down at his station, he began to imagine that table, its texture, its beautiful imperfections, the yellow legal pads on it, giving way at night to carafes of wine and bread and cheese. (In later memory, it became a wooden table instead of one with a glass top.)

In conjunction, Neel had a time-lapse vision of two people gradually falling out of love. As time went by, a thin film of mould would grow over their feelings. After a point, the chasm between them, even when they were holding each other, would be telling, and they'd know it, but they'd think no one else would be the wiser. The tapestry of their lives would change—taken over by a forced calmness, by a bid to stay out of each other's hair, by the coldness (not coolness) of bedsheets, by the barbiturate of television, by the ordinary abyss of children and insipid jobs, by curt messages about practical things, by glances exchanged with friends who could suss out the farce.

Neel did not want a life like that. He wanted pictures that were electrifying; an animalistic love that could spill anywhere and everywhere.

It is during this phase that he became sentimental about fairy lights. He did not have an appropriate place ('home') to put them in yet, but he bought the lights anyway. They would go over snapshots of his future happy life, to make the display of love more pronounced.

The narrow street in the small city where they lived in exile, in a single room, had houses that became part of Neel's pining. One of them was called White House, because the owners had painted the exterior white. Neel's family had been in exile for a year. Neel was still trying to make sense of their despondency. From the street he crossed daily, White House felt like an ocean liner that had set sail. He wanted to see it from inside. He sometimes spotted a young man—Neel would learn later that he was in college—sitting by the window of his room, listening to the hit Hindi film songs of those times. He considered it a luxury—to have a room of one's own, to be able to play music, to have a music system to play it on.

Twenty-five years after that experience—after he had left the street, the city, for good—Neel re-entered the street to revisit the little room that had been their home in exile. At first, the street had felt small and claustrophobic. With time, the perspective, the scale of things, changed. As the car he was in moved slowly, Neel failed to spot White House—to think that while crossing the street every day as a child, he'd prepare to take it in, a hundred metres away!

The fairy lights would have felt so ordinary in White House.

*

Before the idea of solitude at Yale took over—before that time—Neel had no desire to be in America, except to observe it, to see it for the sake of seeing, to get a sense of it, to keep a finger over its pulse. He wanted to write truthfully about it, with a correctness of vision. He wished to get its idiom right.

In essence, he wanted to do America differently from most people he knew; he wanted it to have a whole new gestalt. He wanted his experience not tinged with visits to Costco, iPhone stores, Banana Republics and Times Square. When he was able to go to New York, he was reminded of David Wojnarowicz's magic boxes, with their little shells and model steam trains and watermelon key rings, among other wondrous things.

Once, from Newark airport, a friend picked him up. They drove to a street which was about forty-five minutes away. Dawn had just broken; the friend was supposed to drop him at another friend's house. Mistakenly, he pulled into somebody else's driveway. He became anxious as soon as he realized his error and sped away.

'I don't want someone to shoot us for trespassing,' he said.

Shoot. Trespassing. Neel wondered what Walter Benjamin would have thought of it—people arriving here from different hellish landscapes, through Ellis Island, and now, the same people keeping guns to shoot 'trespassers'.

His main impressions of America, so far, had been of the Empire State Building, which his school textbook had said was the tallest in the world. (The textbook had, in later years, added in an illustration depicting the Boston Tea Party.) Also: John Rambo—Hollywood portrayed him as some sort of Simone Weil. There was, besides this, a faint memory of watching Reagan, talking about Panama, on TV. And, many years later, a man saying, 'Oh my god, oh my god,' as a plane hit the World Trade Center.

America was, to Neel, some country floating in the air, where the president said, 'God bless America,' and seemed to believe that that took care of everything—that the shit the nation hurled around the world would not land in its own backyard.

America—permeating all senses. America—a giant flying saucer, appearing by the horizon of a desert, near a faraway house. America—two soldiers he once saw in Hotel Palestine in Baghdad during the war, which he had gone to cover, scared as rats, drinking Coca-Cola to calm themselves. America—giant food portions. America—wasting too many tissues at Starbucks. America—leather couches and family portraits on the mantle.

The first significant thing Neel did in America was this—he asked a friend to drive him from his house to the grave of Carson McCullers. The graves understood him, he thought; and in this one rested a writer who'd have offered him a sip of dry sherry from her flask, and together they could have sung a ballad at a sad café. It was an October afternoon, and at the entrance of the cemetery, Neel somehow could not find a florist. He walked up to where a man at the cemetery said McCullers rested, and nearby, he found a patch of wild yellow flowers. He picked up one, just one, and walked up to her. And he said, thank you for your life, Miss.

Neel had no idea then that, one day, he'd have to get down a station short of Annie's.

That one day, the sight of flowers would induce in him a dreadful sense of the perishability of all things.

*

As he spends time with Annie at Yale—time that fills him with vitality—he does not know what is to come. The apartment gives him hope that someday he will have a home. It also takes away, at least for then, the ontological dissatisfaction that has ailed him for ages. It is as if home is some long-lost ancestor, and he has been able to, through a séance of sorts, establish contact with it. And it is now speaking to him in a language only he understands.

On that Ikea couch with Annie, it feels like home.

The most vivid memory he has is of waking up there with Annie by his side. It is evening. They returned late in the afternoon and fell asleep. Neel looks out of the window; it is about to get dark. He can hear the organ music at the church. He makes coffee. From his corner, he sees Annie stirring. She knows this is the time of the day when Neel feels low. She groggily starts approaching him wearing his T-shirt, and then, midway, she begins to mock-run towards him, saying, 'Lifeguard coming, lifeguard coming!' And he smiles and holds her close by the window, and they listen together to the music.

It is with Annie that the sense of doom leaves him and he gains calmness. Mid-week, when Annie is likely to be going through a Primo Levi text in her seminar, he goes to Whole Foods to buy the delightful things he has begun to associate with home—apple cider, seedless black grapes, pasta, basil pesto, plain yogurt and different varieties of milk. He waits for the salesgirl to say, 'Twelve o' five,' and 'We are all set,' which means he can swipe his card to pay for his things.

During these months, Neel cooks a lot. For the first time, he identifies with the joy of conjuring up things from raw ingredients, of doling out food in white ceramic plates, and of setting the plates on the table with lilies in a vase.

He begins to ascribe a particular beauty to life, as if the world has suddenly been cured of wars and other ugly things. It is a period of deep intellectual satisfaction. He enjoys the daily rituals of his existence. Everything is joyful—riding a bicycle that he had bought from a medical student who had listed it on Craigslist; wearing binder clips along the bottom of his jeans before hopping on; discovering that a film on David Foster Wallace will be screened in the English department, and, then, going there with Annie, and getting caught in the rain on their way out, and taking shelter in a pub nearby, and ordering two bourbons each and gulping them down, and racing each other back to the apartment, and removing wet clothes in one another's direct gaze, and getting into the bed, bodies intertwined ...

But, sometimes, the tingling sense—that the world he construes as being perfect is far from it—keeps returning. The starkness of the other world, outside the oasis that is Yale, becomes evident in many ways. The moment one walks past Whole Foods, the quality of the sidewalk changes. One can almost feel rage in the air. Listless Black people wearing cheap Costco clothes watch the privileged go by with their bags of organic food. Once a month, he accompanies an Indian couple, friends of his, to an Indian grocery store on the periphery of New Haven. As they pass Black localities in a rented car, he notices people sitting in verandahs, their gaze almost purposeless. Loud music streams out of their houses.

The rage also touches the Yale campus at times, when, suddenly, in the middle of the night, he hears angry voices shouting, 'Fuck' and 'Man, man,' interspersed with police sirens. Out of the window, he sees Black men being taken away. Every second day, mail arrives from the Yale police chief—detailing burglaries or incidents of mugging. These are the mails that Robert had referred to.

The ferment cannot be ignored, but he does not want it to sully his feeling of being provided harbourage. So, he keeps a mental map of only those things and places that have satiated his heart. There is his apartment, the cafés where Annie and he meet, the restaurant owned by the Italian sisters, the library at the law school, where he once heard someone referring to Hillary Clinton as 'snake pants', East Rock hill, and the wooden bench behind Horchow Hall, where he sits in the sun sometimes, reading a book or eating a sandwich.

He also hides the ugliness of America from Father as much as he can. Once, on a Skype call, Neel shows him his boarding pass. Father looks at it and asks, 'So, Mohamed Atta must have used a similar pass?' At that moment, he does not know what to tell him. It is around this time that a terror attack has taken place in Paris. On the call, with a quivering voice, Father asks him to stay away from concert halls.

Neel tries to show Father all the good things. On video calls, he reveals to him how visiting scholar apartments look; the enormity of buildings all around; how nobody honks on roads (except in Manhattan!). He sends him pictures of stacks of food in departmental stores; he tells him how there is order everywhere and how everyone waits in queue. He does not tell him about Ferguson. He does not tell him about the 'Mister, Mister, one dollar, Mister!' calls around street corners. He tries to create a picture-perfect America. Let there be one place in this world that Father can make his peace with, Neel tells himself. Despite the rose-tinted spectacles he offers, Father remembers Mohamed Atta; despite all his reassurances, Father seems to intuitively know that paradise can come crashing down in a moment.

And then it does—the one that could have been possible with Annie.

*

After he returns from Yale, in the beginning, he tries not to think too much of Annie. He hopes to replicate a big part of his life at Yale in Delhi. It is like one of those BuzzFeed stories—a house, in one part of the world, plucked from its base by a helicopter, and placed somewhere else.

But a week in, the impossibility of his endeavour hits him. The base of his life in Delhi has a very different design; the house begins to feel wobbly. The problem, he realizes, is fundamental, and this nixes his attempts at building a meta-life of scholarship, of reading and writing. The odour of the house help's quick and heartless cooking, the merciless banging of utensils in the sink, wear him down. He gets sucked into taking care of mundane things that need attention continually—online payments, water purifiers gone kaput, making calls to service centres where young people say, 'Is there anything else I can help you with?' even when they know that they are in no position to help. Then, there are things that topple over any possibility of an idyll—Father's feeble voice on the phone every time he says he will be late, the idiotic honking at traffic signals even before the lights turn green, articles on politics with the same ideological spin, the fake air kisses and the emotional baggage of acquaintances.

*

In the night, he can hear sounds from a party somewhere in his neighbourhood. It transports him to the time when he had gone with Annie to a house party in New Haven.

He can see it still: a tipsy elderly scholar looking at them and saying, 'So, you two are an item?' Then, he lights a cigarette from its wrong end. Annie is amused that they have been called an item. It brings colour to her cheeks. It is a full moon night. Annie wears a blue cardigan over a dress. The scholar goes back into the host's house, and Neel takes a stroll with Annie in the quiet neighbourhood.

Annie's hand is in his. He thinks: not a soul is out. He imagines how Annie and he will look together in old age. He thinks of certain apartments in New York, belonging to writers—one of these could be their home. He pictures what will happen when a journalist comes to interview them—the ritual of removing the jacket and keeping it in a closet next to the main door. He conjures up the back of other apartments, visible from their window; the kitchen slab; the daily practice of washing utensils, while the other person wipes them dry.

Or: he pictures the two of them in a Midwest town, the kind where young people are restless and always want to get out. Annie and he are exceptions; they are embedded in the community. They know the sheriff, and the sheriff knows them, and they call each other by their first names, and they do barbecues together.

*

Two months without Annie. Two months without being an item.

Outside, the city sounds as if it is in the throes of a civil war. Everyone is in a hurry to reach somewhere, even if it means disregarding the rules of traffic and civility. Every movement, every action is reckless; and because it is reckless, it feels oppressive.

Neel has done so much running in the last two months that he has lost five kilos. The pain that ultra-running causes is the only thing that keeps the pain of Annie's absence in check. His old running buddies, with whom he had spent years in training, are happy to see him back. But they also notice that he is avoiding training with the group. Instead of early mornings, he trains later in the day. On the main arterial road in the city, as the young employees of multinational companies, wearing their access cards around their necks, come out for cigarette and tea breaks, he whizzes past like a ghost. On the route there are two flower shops next to each other. In February, their supplies are overflowing. He runs even faster. He is running against the traffic flow, and from their cars, people look at him as if he is some maniac. He runs to empty his head, but that also fails to work.

He remembers eating a meal next to the African violets. He remembers Annie's feverish body. He remembers the café, and the tuna sandwich, and the sisters at the Italian restaurant, and the timbre of the air outside, and the million hues of Annie's hair. He recalls the sound of her jeans slithering up her slender legs, as she rushes to her class.

Every day, he wakes up with the resolve that today will be better. His last book, on the war in India's hinterland, had been published more than five years ago; he needs to begin on another one. The resolve to work on it dissipates within moments. By afternoon, he has given up on the day; he promises himself that he will be the perfect man tomorrow.

But his days are marred with the same repetitiveness. There is no *now*; he is either wallowing in the past or imagining future catastrophes. He tries to read, but he cannot focus; he absorbs nothing. For inspiration, he turns to author interviews in the *Paris Review*; little moves him.

There is no method to his pursuits. The only constant is this—he wastes precious hours. He makes lists, but none of the things that matter come to fruition. He deletes all apps from his mobile phone, then reinstalls them.

To make matters worse, a strange pain in his lower abdomen, that had appeared and vanished of its own volition a few years ago, has now returned with a vengeance. It is because of his long, arduous journeys through the hinterland; also because his mind is continuously playing, on its zoetrope, the terrible things he has witnessed. This has left an imprint on the body, like a bad conscience.

It keeps him awake at night.

He knows that Father can sense that he is struggling with something. But he does not ask Neel directly; one day, though, he expresses concern about his sunken cheeks. 'Running is fine, but you don't have to run so much that you will simply disappear,' he says.

It could be called Father's intervention. With it also comes the realization that Neel must go back to writing. So, he pauses his running frenzy; he implores himself to set a writing routine.

He tries establishing this at a nearby café—he visits it every morning, taking with him, in a bag, books and notebooks, and a box containing all kinds of pens and pencils. In the early hours, the café is nearly empty, and in a few days, he warms up; he starts to write half a page or so. By late morning or afternoon, however, the café's white-noise reverie gets disrupted by people from nearby offices and by bored Korean housewives whose husbands manage businesses in the industrial areas. Sometimes, he is late and they arrive before he does. On occasions like this, he receives a call from Kim.

'They are here,' she whispers, one day, even as he hears the din regular customers raise behind her.

Kim runs the café with a menagerie of young people on the cusp of adulthood. They have been entrusted to her by the social welfare department. They come from households where they have known abuse in one form or another. She trains them and lets them gain valuable work experience in the café, after which they are absorbed as part of the workforce of big hotels.

Now that the café is ruled out, Neel doesn't know what to do. He is out, so he takes a walk in the shopping arcade across the café. The apartments and markets in the vicinity, named by semi-literate builders intent on aping the West, make him laugh.

There are a few benches around the arcade's fountain. In the evening, these get crowded, but at this hour, in the April sun, the crowds are thin; the benches are mostly empty, except for one or two occupied by pedicurists in black salon uniforms, fighting or flirting with their lovers on the phone. Neel looks around for the elderly woman, who comes by herself, buys a chicken patty from Sugar & Spice, and takes small bites, totally immersed in the act. The heat does not seem to affect her at all. She wipes her mouth carefully with a napkin, throws it into the bin and walks away slowly, as if her legs are filled with sand.

Today, the old woman isn't around. Neel watches as the world passes by. If he were in Yale, by this time, he'd have left his apartment in New Haven, with the promise of meeting Annie.

The thought of Annie makes Neel want to leave. As he checks his phone, there is a news flash about the death of Prince in Minnesota. An old memory of Adaa comes to him—they are at a hotel in Bali, when someone gets up and begins to sing 'Purple Rain'. He remembers Adaa raising her arms to the tune, as she and others join the singing.

He walks towards his house—past colonies; across a park where he had once fought with a woman who was shooing away the children of sweepers from the swing; past the metro line, the hospital chains and the gypsies selling fake aphrodisiacs—and approaches the gate of his society. There is a line of delivery boys waiting to enter the society; some are simply taking a brief rest under a cluster of trees.

He spots a woman standing outside his building and feels as if he has seen her somewhere. As he comes closer, the woman smiles at him. It is then that he knows.

'Gurupriya,' he says. He holds her by the arm. 'Why didn't you go up?'

'I knew you were not there.'

'How?'

'I just felt it.'

'What if I had not returned? What if ...'

She puts her hand on his mouth.

'For someone who believes in god, you ask too many questions.'

*

Neel had little understanding of the countryside when he began his life in Delhi.

He vaguely knew that there were three major theatres of conflict in the country. One was in the north—it had put him in exile. Another was in the northeast, which remained farthest from the consciousness of Delhi. And then, there were the central and eastern parts, that drew him in and gave him a body of experience.

Most Indians had scant knowledge about the heart of the country. They read of it only occasionally in newspapers, or heard of it on radio or in TV news bulletins, when the guerrillas attacked government forces. The rebellion against the state was led by people inspired by Mao; they had named themselves after a village, where the first insurrection had taken place in the late '60s, almost ten years before Neel was born. At that time, it had been quelled, but now it had reappeared in a different form and had spread rather quietly, led by men and women who mostly came from urban areas—teachers, engineers, social activists. Moved by the oppression they witnessed in society, they got radicalized—some, while in college; others, after getting inspired by something as simple as a revolutionary song.

At the time when Neel started work in Delhi, not many cared about the conflict in India's hinterland. If Neel got drawn to it, it was by fate—in part, propelled by the desire to run away from the tribalism of journalists and intellectuals; but also because of a chance meeting.

There was a man who took Neel to the heart of this world. Neel had always been lucky in that sense; men, older than him, who saw things and understood them, recognized his restlessness. They never explicitly pointed it out to him, but he was aware that they perceived his struggle to change the course of his life.

The man was twenty years older than Neel. They had first met many years ago. It was a strange way of meeting. After the exile, Neel's entire energy had been focused on finding a way of getting out of the small city his family inhabited. It took him some time, but he managed to secure admission in Chandigarh, in Panjab University. In the first year, he became part of a group doing relief work in the state—over the monsoons, there had been unprecedented rain, and the rivers had breached their banks, destroying bridges, ruining roads. The water had entered villages, mauling crops and spreading disease. A few volunteers, including Neel, went around in a van, distributing rice, flour and sugar across affected villages.

It was hot and humid. On their second or third day, they had been working all morning; late in the afternoon, they paused for a quick lunch comprising bread, potatoes and pickle. Neel finished hurriedly and stepped out of the compound to wash his hands.

In front of the compound, there was a house, and beside that, a small clearing that led to fields that spread all the way to the horizon. He was walking alone in that direction when, in front of some barbed wire that acted as a fence for the flooded fields, he came across a small stone memorial with something written in Gurmukhi. There was a sooty earthen lamp before it that hadn't been lit in a long time. Neel stood there, intrigued.

'This is a martyr's memorial,' a voice said from behind.

As Neel turned, he found a man wearing a pale yellow bush shirt and trousers. He had starting balding from the front and was wearing thick glasses, behind which his eyes shone. That was the first thing that held Neel—his eyes, the whites of his eyes, more precisely. The man had spoken in Punjabi, but when he took a closer look at Neel, he switched to Hindi.

'Where have you come from?' the man asked.

Neel was thrilled to meet someone from outside his life in college (where hardly any curiosity, other than to do with women and motorbikes, could be satisfied). He had never had a chance to talk to someone like this, serendipitously; he was genuinely interested in knowing about his life.

'Do you live here?' Neel asked, after answering his question.

He could see that the man was trying to arrive at an appropriate answer. 'I have no home, but yes, I have been living here for some time,' he said.

Neel left it at that, but the man told him more about the stone memorial. In the 1960s, he said, there had been a revolution. The word itself crackled on his tongue. By revolution, the man meant the peasant movement in Bengal, which had become violent in Naxalbari. Young men and women, who wanted to overthrow the feudal system, had chosen violence. They were called Naxals.

So, the 'revolution' had touched these parts as well, where the man and Neel now stood. In these parts, there was a tradition of suffixing the names of people (like the one whose memorial they stood in front of) with 'Kaamrade'—Comrade—as a marker of faith in Communist ideology. Preceding this was a nickname. The memorial was dedicated to Sukhi Kaamrade, who had shot dead a police officer with a rifle that belonged to his father. The officer's son had chased him right afterwards on a horse and had shot him just as he reached the periphery of his village, at the spot where the memorial was built later.

Both Neel and the man stood there, bonding over a memory that was now as much Neel's as the man's. But, in Neel's instance, it was a small snapshot of a much larger picture to which he had no access.

In the distance, he could hear the other volunteers walking back to resume work. He was wanted there. Gurnaam—that was the man's name—asked him for his address, and he wrote it down with a cheap ballpoint pen across the flap of a pack of Charminar cigarettes. (This, Neel learnt later, was the preferred brand for all those who believed in the idea of a revolution; it was a small way to collectivize.)

Neel left Gurnaam at the spot and rushed back to where the volunteers were distributing ration supplies. The relief work continued for a few more days across villages.

Three weeks later, on a dull evening, Neel was washing clothes in the hostel bathroom, when a mate shouted that he had a visitor. Neel put on a shirt and went downstairs. In the darkness of the corridor below, where the tube light had broken days ago, on a wooden bench, he saw Gurnaam sitting with a boy who was only a few years older than Neel. Gurnaam got up when he saw Neel, smiled, shook his hand with both hands, and hugged him. He exuded warmth, and an invitation of openness, of friendship. The tall, lanky boy with him had a helmet in his hands. His name was Jaswant, or Jassi Kaamrade; he was a master's student at the university and lived in a hostel on campus.

Neel didn't know it then—but it was at this moment that he held firmly to the chance that the universe had thrown at him. Fate wants us to stay in orbit, but out of some larger covenant with an invisible force, it is also duty-bound to send a rope our way, so we can chart a new trajectory. It is for us to grasp the rope … or not. Years later, with the benefit of hindsight, Neel could see that he had indeed grasped it. In fact, he always took the rope—except in matters of love. When he loved, he let the rope go.

This rope, the rope Gurnaam had thrown at him that day, opened up a world he felt deeply curious about. Gurnaam said that he had brought Jassi along so that Neel knew he had friends here. 'If you have a problem, reach out to Jassi,' he said. As they spoke, Neel felt that Jassi was looking at him intently, as if trying to gauge if he was worth his time. They went out nearby and Gurnaam ordered tea from a shack. Jassi spoke in between using English words—not sentences, but words. Neel remembered 'legacy' (of Partition), and 'class', and what Jassi called 'structural violence'. Before they left, Jassi opened his torn bag and handed over a book to him. It was *Mother* by Gorky—Neel had never heard of him.

'Read it,' Gurnaam said. 'And if you have any questions, ask.'

'How do I meet you again?'

'I will be in touch,' he said, and held his arm for a moment.

Over the next few months, Jassi and Neel met several times. Gradually, he read other books. His circle of comrades widened. They gave him a Hindi translation of the poet Pash, who had been assassinated by Sikh extremists in the '80s for his opposition to the idea of a separate Sikh homeland. His work resonated deeply with Neel. One of his poems averred that being filled with a deathly silence was the most dangerous of things. (Many years later, Neel went to Pash's house, where the poet had scribbled on a table: 'Know what how why'. It lay gathering dust.)

Every third day, the comrades gave him a new book. The first that Gurnaam offered was Fanon's *The Wretched of the Earth*. He wondered how the comrades got hold of these books in English, even though they had only rudimentary knowledge of the language. They would speak in Hindi for Neel's benefit, but after a few minutes, they'd unknowingly switch back to Punjabi. Slowly, he became used to it, learning to infer the meaning of conversations through catchwords—thanks to which, he would remember discussions that lasted through the night.

In the beginning, he was a spectator, as the comrades held debates on politics; these often became heated. There was a big debate on police action in the state against Sikh extremists fighting for a separate homeland. The comrades were divided on the nature of insurgencies; they had a romantic notion about insurrections. But the insurgency in Punjab, that had killed hundreds of innocent civilians, had forced them to reconsider their stand. Some of them then turned against the Sikh extremists, and in the process many comrades like Pash were killed. The comrades were not clear about the circumstances behind the exodus Neel's family had faced; so they did not get into a debate with Neel over the issue or openly endorse it. In their conversations, a few names came up very often, and some strange places he had not heard of, and that he would never come across in the daily pile of newspapers he read at the state library.

His other friends in college knew nothing about his meetings with Gurnaam and the rest. Gurnaam came often and stayed in Jassi's room.

One evening, Neel went to the university campus to meet Jassi. He knocked at his door, but no one responded. He checked the door, but it was not locked. Maybe Jassi was asleep. But, surely, he would have woken up by now? Just as Neel was about to turn back, a man's voice called from inside: 'Who is it?' Neel replied that he was Jassi's friend. After a pause, the door opened and he saw a bespectacled man in an undershirt and pyjamas, his eyes red. He let Neel in. He sat on the cot, while Neel sat on the chair. On one side of the room, he saw a bag. After a little while, Jassi returned with Gurnaam, whom he had gone to pick up from the bus stand. The bespectacled man was introduced to him as 'Doctor'.

'Doctor of what?'

Gurnaam laughed. 'Doctor of the poor people!'

From his experience with the comrades, Neel knew that they left some things unsaid. This was their way, and he accepted it.

That night, they opened a bottle of rum. Jassi got some packets of snacks and these were arranged on a newspaper placed on the floor. The four of them sat around it. They poured Neel a small drink. It was an initiation of some sort. He took one sip and felt it travel through his throat and chest like fire. But he did not want to appear weak or rude. Gurnaam asked if he was okay, and he lied and said, yes. They drank in Doctor's honour, who, they said, had returned from a long journey. Neel knew better than to ask more questions. By this time, he was also worried about how he was going to finish the contents of his glass—it tasted like pesticide.

Fifteen minutes later, he became sweaty and, on touching his chin, found that he could not feel it at all. Jassi and Doctor were deep in conversation; the word 'DK' came up repeatedly. They spoke of check dams, malaria, and the need for equipment for blood tests. At one point, Doctor looked at Gurnaam and told him that he was wanted in 'DK'. Gurnaam did not respond; his eyes remained fixed on his glass.

It felt good to be there, among these odd men, who were, in a way, friends, and who trusted him, and did not ask anything from him. Many months later, Neel opened up to Gurnaam about what his family had faced before and after the exodus. The confession had been triggered by a comrade, who opposed police action in Punjab and eulogized the killing of civilians, calling this 'class action'. Neel felt an outburst building within him and told the comrade that it was murder and that not everything could be justified in the name of a revolution.

That night, Gurnaam took Neel aside and said he wanted to hear his story. This was when Neel told him about the mayhem preceding his family's departure, the jeers heard at mosques, the taunts encountered on roads, the killings, the difficulties of being in exile, what it meant to live as a refugee. That night, Gurnaam used a word in Punjabi to empathize with him. He said he understood his 'peedh'—the pain; in this case, the ache associated with losing a home. Neel could not articulate his inability to centre himself, to feel 'at home' in any place, including the one from which he had been exiled. But they had crossed a river, and he felt closer to Gurnaam than to the others.

Gurnaam also told him something he made a mental note of: 'The weakness of the movement is that it has no space or tolerance for individual stories. It only understands, and is a reaction to, things that happen in a sweep. There is some work happening for the poorest of the poor. It is not perfect, but it is something.'

Gurnaam paused, then added, 'I also ignore things. The movement is paranoid; it does not trust anyone. But that is the nature of it. Nothing can be done.'

Gurnaam told Neel that sometimes he felt 'wrong things' were happening. When they became too much to handle, when they weighed on his conscience, he took a step back. With time, he reconciled. 'The day I don't, I will end myself,' Gurnaam said.

'You mean you will end your association with the comrades?'

Gurnaam looked at him and smiled. 'Yes,' he said.

After some time, Gurnaam disappeared, and Neel did not see him for weeks.

So, this became his life with his new friends. Gurnaam returned, and then Jassi was gone. Sometimes, he would find new people in Jassi's room. At one point, Doctor disappeared. Neel had seen him twice in the hostel.

Neel would meet him again some years later—however, in very different circumstances.

*

Neel first came to Delhi a few months after their exodus from Kashmir. This was around two years before he met Gurnaam in Punjab.

A cousin had developed hernia that required surgery; her doctor in the small city said she would have to be taken to the capital. A surgeon had been suggested, whose Delhi address was provided. The cousin's family wanted Neel's household to come along. They had no idea about how things worked in big cities, but more people meant more ways of figuring stuff out.

The cousin's family began preparing for the journey. With each passing minute, it became obvious how unaware they were of the larger world. They packed rice, mustard oil, pulses, even a giant pestle to grind condiments in. The household items were carried in bundles and bags that filled the entire overhead bin of the overnight bus they were supposed to take. Once they were seated, the bus—called a 'video coach' because it played films—did not move. Insurgency was at its peak in Punjab, and sometimes, buses would be stopped and Hindu passengers singled out and shot dead. It was only after sunrise the next day that the bus commenced its journey.

They passed through dusty towns and villages, and for the first time, Neel saw rivers he had read of only in school textbooks. They crossed a city he had heard his parents mention so many times: Amritsar. It was here that a British general had opened fire on Indian protestors, killing over a thousand of them. His parents spoke of the Golden Temple and a famous Hindu shrine in the city. But: Jallianwala Bagh—did they visit it? Did they feel any connection with its history? Did it cause a murmur in their hearts?

It was late when they reached Old Delhi. The chaos! The bus was immediately surrounded by touts and beggars and coolies and taxi- and autorickshaw-drivers (and, later, they were told, pickpockets). Of the next few minutes, Neel would form no memory, except that it was a miracle that somehow all of them—they were bundled into different autorickshaws—ended up together at the same place, a small hotel near the New Delhi railway station.

The next morning, as Father and his uncle left to find the doctor and make arrangements for the cousin's surgery, Neel went to the rooftop of the hotel to pass time. He watched the people on the streets below.

One day, he heard a strange, rhythmic noise—similar to the times when a man would come to their house in Kashmir with a strange instrument. It was used to shred pieces of cotton that had turned lumpy inside quilts, after which the cotton was refilled, making the quilts firmer. He looked down, unable to locate the source of the sound. After a few seconds, he zeroed in on it. A man, his face painted like a monkey, and wearing a false tail, was whipping himself, walking with a peculiar strut, as if his ankles had been chained. Around him, people were going about their business.

A man had to whip himself in order to be able to eat here. Neel had not been exposed to this idea before, and for days, the recollection disturbed him.

Six years after that first experience, Neel took another overnight bus (this time, it left at night) to begin a new life in Delhi. Now, he was armed with an education outside the classroom, thanks to Gurnaam. Initially, he lived near a cinema hall that had shut down for renovation. There was a legend around it—apparently, it had been won by a wrestler in a gambling match. The wrestler's sons had then studied abroad and learnt new ways of making money. They were turning the cinema hall into the city's first multiplex.

The cinema hall was situated in the middle of a market complex. There was a news agency in the vicinity, from where Neel would buy the *Economic and Political Weekly*. There was also a McDonald's, with Ronald, the clown, resting on a bench by the main door. In the evening, the place transformed, with young lovers sitting in a row on circular stone benches, along a passageway on one side of the complex.

Neel had spent the past year reading Simone Weil, and this had awakened in him a deep sense of life. He wanted to live with a clear rigour, with honesty. Without sounding too desperate, he longed to remain vulnerable to goodness, to love, to the idea of home—words that, to his mind, amounted to the same thing. Beyond this, he had very few definitive ideas.

A girl, who wore beautiful skirts, was a regular at the market. She'd come with her lover, and they'd sit at their usual spot by one of the roundabouts. She'd always carry a string of jasmine flowers in her hands. It was a ritual of sorts. A bunch of urchins would sell these flowers to young couples who gathered for a private moment. After the woman would seat herself, the lover would get a bag of popcorn. Then, they'd talk—Neel imagined this—about how their day had gone. It was tough living in the city; to keep one's head above water. In a poem written in Delhi in 1954, the poet Agyeya had addressed a snake. How—when it had never become civilized or come to live in the city—had it learnt to bite? From where did it get its poison? In the darkness of those evenings, surrounded by the fragrance of jasmines, the man and his beloved did not have to mull over such questions. There was love, and it had continuity, permanence.

After some days, Neel got a job with a small newspaper. He would start early and finish late at night. On his way back, he'd sometimes stop at the complex. By this time, the lovers would be gone. He'd find the flower-selling urchins either eating leftovers or sniffing glue. Only a cigarette kiosk would be open, along with a few eateries.

Neel did not remember when exactly—it must have been two months after securing a job—he left work early and decided to go to the complex. He bought cigarettes and sat at his usual place, reading Weil's *The Need for Roots*. He was absorbed in the book and did not realize how much time had passed. When he looked up, he found the girl at her usual spot. Perhaps her lover would be coming any time now. But more time passed and she remained alone. Her back was towards him but he could see her head was bent. He felt as if she were surrounded by a circle of sadness. He was shy about approaching her, but he also felt compelled to. He first walked past her, heading to the popcorn stall, where he bought a packet. As he walked back, he stopped near her with a jerk, like he had suddenly seen her. She looked up; they had never spoken before, but she had seen him there, too.

He smiled. 'Where is your friend?'

There was a pause. 'We are no longer together,' she said.

These are the saddest lines, like that Neruda poem.

Neel stood there for a few seconds, and then he gave her the packet of popcorn; she accepted it silently. He left her alone.

'No longer' became a dreadful thing in his head. That's why when Annie said, 'We are one now, we are one,' it made him joyous. Then: 'no longer' struck.

Three days after that evening, Neel went back. He waited, but the girl did not appear. The next week, too, she was not there. And the next month as well. Then, he moved out of the neighbourhood.

*

Work in Delhi kept Neel busy. But Gurnaam remained in touch. His letters would come more frequently than Neel was able to respond. He often enclosed cuttings of newspapers and journals that he must have felt would be of benefit to Neel. A few times, they also met when Gurnaam visited Delhi, where he had friends like Jassi in the university. He'd stay with a scholar in one of the hostels. He did not venture out very much. 'It is better this way,' he said.

Two years had passed, when Neel got a call from Gurnaam at the newspaper office where he was working.

'Will you come and see me?' he asked in his soft, stable voice.

Gurnaam had instructed Neel never to mention the name of the place they'd meet at; it was an understanding that they would always convene here, in Connaught Place, on a bench, next to which an old man sold iron boats that, due to a small miracle of physics, could move in a bowl of water.

When he reached, he found Gurnaam eating roasted gram from a paper bag. He survived on these things, but mostly on tea and cigarettes.

'Hello, Mr Journalist,' he said, while hugging Neel.

They sat there, next to each other, as Gurnaam offered him the roasted gram. It was evening; a huge number of people, returning from offices, cut through the park to save themselves the trouble of taking a longer, more circuitous route.

'Look at them, not one is smiling,' Gurnaam said. He was right. Later, he'd keep testing his observation of the day. As he stood by Delhi roads, he looked at the faces of people in buses and in shared autos—haggard, unhappy.

Neel inquired about Jassi; Gurnaam said he had enrolled in a PhD programme.

'It is time for you to see things,' he suddenly said.

An event was taking place in DK, he told him. The name revealed itself to Neel at last. It stood for Dandakaranya, the guerrilla zone in India's heart, where the writ of the comrades ran large. That month, two big rebel groups were coming together in alliance; Gurnaam said it was a big victory for the revolutionary forces. 'It will change you,' he asserted.

After that, he left.

Fifteen days after the meeting with Gurnaam, Neel was in an overnight train to Hyderabad. From there, a bus took him to a tiny town, a journey of about five hours. He checked into a small hotel. A day before his departure from Delhi, some instructions had been sent to him. These included the name of this accommodation. After checking out the next morning at 6 a.m., he was asked to stand near a pillar at the local bus stand. He was to carry a book in his hand. If no one came for thirty minutes, he was to return to his hotel and check in again. At 6 p.m., he was to go once more and stand by the bus stand. If still nobody came, he was to return to Delhi.

That night at the hotel, he could not sleep. He was excited; besides, there were too many mosquitoes, unperturbed by the coil that the hotel manager had handed to him at the reception. Gurnaam had warned him of these micro-predators. Before leaving, he had, at his behest, popped a dose of Mefloquine, that made his body heat up for days. But it was supposed to offer protection from malaria, which, Gurnaam said, was endemic there.

The next morning, he walked out, passing the reception area, where a young man wrapped in a dirty blanket snored heavily. It took him about fifteen minutes to get to the bus stand. It was deserted, except for some beggars who were still sleeping and a few ragpickers who were collecting the remains of the previous night.

As he stood there, a beggar came and mumbled something to him in what he thought was Telugu. In his naiveté, he believed the beggar was his guide. But he left Neel alone. Twenty minutes later, a man arrived. He came straight to Neel and nodded. Then, he turned and started walking back towards where he had come from. Neel followed him.

In a lane, another man was waiting on a bike. By way of hand gestures, Neel was asked to sit behind him. The two men exchanged a few words, which he did not understand, and then the biker and Neel were off. After a few minutes, they were on some highway. It was mostly empty, except for small groups of men carrying ropes and earthen pitchers in their hands. These, he came to know later, were men who collected sap from a particular tree in the area to make alcohol. He noticed that the people around him looked markedly different. They were no longer those whom the North Indians, in their geographical ignorance, collectively called South Indians. These were tribals, or Adivasis, for whom the geographical markers of north and south were irrelevant. This was where they lived, on land that belonged to them. On the highway up ahead, he saw some of the Adivasi women sitting on their haunches, not by the corner of the road but on the road itself. He feared that a passing vehicle would come and mow them down. He tried speaking to his companion in Hindi and English, but the man did not respond, his body remained stiff and his focus stayed on the drive ahead.

They travelled for an hour or so, after which they stopped at a small room by the roadside. There was a mountain of dug-up earth beside it and a tree stump with vulcanized tyres around. He noticed signboards advertising a coal mine. The room held a motor repair workshop. The biker was gone. But someone else came and handed him a glass of over-sweetened tea. After a few minutes, another man appeared and shook Neel's hand, saying, 'Welcome,' and 'We go now.' Neel gulped down the remaining tea and followed the man outside, where another bike awaited them, and they continued their journey.

At some point, they were taken in a trolley pulled by a tractor down a stone-strewn path. After that, the only way forward was on foot. It was around sunset that they reached the outskirts of what looked like a deep forest. There was so much humidity; white patches, caused by the salt he had lost through sweat, appeared on his trousers. To the right, he caught sight of a few people walking in a neat column towards him. They moved solemnly, as if leading a hearse. They were all wearing military fatigues, and as they came closer, he noticed that these were too loose for their thin bodies. There were four men, and leading them was a woman. Only she carried an AK-47; the others had swung across their bodies battered .303 rifles. The woman raised her fist in what Neel would come to recognize as the revolutionary greeting, which, for the next several years, he would become so used to that he would greet friends in the city like that. This woman, it turned out, could speak in English.

This woman was M.

*

There was a pattern to the day. He was put up in a camp in the middle of a dense forest. It was nothing but tarpaulin sheets held in place by ropes, under which he lay on similar sheets spread on the ground. Everything was in a constant state of flurry—people coming and going all the time. There was a small school run for new recruits. On its other side were a few tents occupied by women guerrillas. In the evening, after military drills, they combed their hair, laughed, and told each other secrets. A handful of them were fierce-looking; he had never seen them smile. A woman, who was with him like a shadow, turned out to be one of M's bodyguards.

The thing that struck him on the first night was the purity of sound—no whirr of kitchen appliances, or hum of air conditioners, no car alarms, no tring-tring of landline phones, no screeching sound of teleprinters in the newsroom. The night was deep ink; there was no electricity, there were no bright artificial lights. All he could hear in the dark was the whine of the cicadas and strange bird calls he had never encountered before. By day, he was met with smiles that carried the guilelessness of those who dwelt in these forests. No deceit, no false earnestness. They smiled when they really had to. They spoke little, and when they did, it was without any falseness in their voice.

These were people cut off from the state's largesse. In a way, they had nothing; they did not know that there was something they had a right to and that it had been denied to them. The guerrillas, who had read books and military manuals, were there to tell them what they deserved and that the only way of getting this was through the barrel of the gun. About Mao, the Adivasis had no clue. That there was a government, a prime minister, a parliament responsible for their welfare was also not a concept they were familiar with. They had a unique relationship with the universe—one that had remained unchanged ever since man had come into being. They lived on forest resources; the trees were their gods. They plucked what they wanted to; they hunted in the same way their ancestors had hundreds of years ago. They drank from their rivers. When they felt unwell, they would go to a man they considered to be god's representative, or his messenger, someone in touch with spirits they could not see. They did not know that he could not do much for them. A fever would grip their bodies and they would die. Sometimes, they died because the soldiers from the mainland were frustrated and would kill them on suspicion of helping Maoists. The Maoists would do the same thing. The women would grieve in a silent way over the dead bodies. They would sit, or stand, their arms raised behind their heads, their faces contorted. The deceased would then be buried in a clearing outside their habitation. The cots and battered utensils that the dead had been using while alive would be kept next to their places of burial. And so, life would go on. In times of birth, of death, of in-betweenness, there was a brew made from flowers that a tree god had left for them.

Over the years, there had been a rupture to their way of life. The nation state needed wealth and found that there was an abundance of natural resources in this region. So, men arrived and their heavy machinery arrived; incense was lit, ribbons were cut, gods were invoked. And the wealth-building began in earnest. The people who walked barefoot over such wealth were not beneficiaries of the extraction. They saw men—traders from towns and cities—taking it all away. With these men came the petty representatives of the state—the policemen, the forest guards. Suddenly, the forest—their home and livelihood for centuries—became out of bounds. It also changed; the rivers carried water that looked like blood.

As the city inched close, with it came its monstrosity, its greed, the poison that Agyeya had referred to. Nothing was enough. More, more, more—the collective voice rose. Outside the forests, new temples were built—dams and IITs.

At some point in the '80s, the guerrillas arrived. They had a plan in mind—to establish a rear base, where they could go into hiding when the state came after them. This was a lesson they had learnt from their earlier failure in the late 1960s and early 1970s. Soon enough, they realized that they could create their governance model right here. At first, the Adivasis ran away from them. They were naturally inclined to stay away from outsiders. But as the 'outsiders' started making minor differences to their existence—scaring away greedy traders, beating up lecherous land officials, making check dams and offering medicine to prevent malaria—they came to be looked upon with a degree of trust. The little measures taken by guerrillas should have woken up the state and brought in its benevolence. But instead, it brought further ugliness—a fact that pushed the Adivasis towards the guerrillas.

Now, the guerrillas wanted to take control, which meant that the region had to become inaccessible to outside influence. They started bringing down whatever infrastructure for electricity that had been laid down by the state here, and destroyed roads, even those on the periphery. DK was a large contiguous area extending across several states, and now the guerrillas operated their system of governance here. This was their own country.

It was this system, this country, that Neel had been invited to see. The hollow left by the state stunned him. His own story, his own feelings—all of these felt petty. He had never been exposed to this kind of poverty, or to human invisibilization of this degree.

He stayed for a week, mostly under M's charge.

Every day, he was taken to see one project or the other, run by the guerrillas: the little school, the medical camp, the pond where the guerrillas had started pisciculture, the fields where uniformed rebels toiled along with the villagers. Neel interacted with M, but it did not go past what she wanted him to know. He asked her about her life, but she said it did not matter. As someone committed to the idea of revolution, her personal story held no value. He tried a few journalistic tricks, but she wouldn't budge.

One day, while there was a lull in the activities in the afternoon, he found her sitting by the entrance of a villager's hut. In front of her was a child, who had a gash on his knee. The blood had attracted flies, and M was cleaning it. As he stood there, she took out a bottle of Neosporin from her kit and dabbed it on the wound. Then she said something to the child in their language. As the child walked away to play, Neel sat by her.

'I need your help,' he said.

She looked at him.

'I have seen the things that the party wanted me to see. But I want to understand from you a few things that go beyond showing me the picture-book perfection of your movement.'

She smiled. 'What do you want to know?'

'Tell me what you saw the first time you came to DK.'

She kept looking at him; he looked back at her. Then she turned her face towards the forest which lay in front of them.

'By the time I arrived, the comrades were already here. But they were still struggling. The area, as you can see, is vast. And the Adivasis were extremely wary of outsiders. Every now and again, let us say once a year or so, a hunting tribe would attack the Adivasis' hamlets to take away whatever little they found—goats or roosters. The Adivasis had a resigned approach to this, as if it were inevitable. They accepted what came. They'd vanish into the forest and return once the raid was over. The outsiders—like the hunting tribes, or the town traders coming to take tamarind and other valuable forest produce, or the forest guards, or the land officials—were not necessarily evil. But there was an important human lesson to learn there.'

'And what lesson was that?'

'The lesson was that if given a chance, a man will take advantage of another man weaker than him. This I understood very quickly here.'

Suddenly, Neel saw her getting alert. He looked where she was looking but could not see anything. Two heartbeats later, she relaxed again. From the other end of the forest, two uniformed girls appeared. As they came closer, M shouted at them. They stood fixed in one spot, and after M must have asked them to leave, they broke into a jog and were gone.

'They are not supposed to come from that side,' M said. Then, she continued, 'After I came to these forests, I began interacting with the women here. And I saw that many of them had children but were not married. And stranger still, the children had names that were not native to the Adivasis. As I got more involved, I came to see that all kinds of outsiders had exploited these women. The outsiders had named the children like they'd name their own offspring back home. The only difference being—they abandoned Adivasi woman and child.'

'So, what are you trying to do here?' Neel asked.

'You know, in college, in English class, we had précis writing. The précis of what we are trying here is this—we are telling the Adivasis that they deserve better. And we are teaching them to fight for it.'

*

On his last night, the guerrillas had organized a little feast for the Adivasis. It was the day of their deity, and the guerrillas took care not to disturb harmless cultural practices. Wearing military fatigues, the guerrillas, both men and women, held hands with the Adivasis and danced to the rhythmic beat of drums. At one point, when the drumbeats had reached a crescendo, M's bodyguard pulled Neel into the dance. Neel was clumsy at first, but soon, he became one with the rhythm and danced late into the night. It was just a dance, but for Neel, that night, it signified resistance, it meant charting one's own passage—an idea that Neel himself was deeply familiar with.

It must have been after midnight that the dance ended. As the group broke, Neel walked to a side and lay on the ground. His shirt was plastered to his body with sweat. He had begun to smell now because it was not always possible to take a bath. As he looked up, he was struck by the beauty of the Milky Way, which he was seeing for the first time. He closed his eyes, and the rose bushes of his childhood swirled in his consciousness.

After he returned, Neel felt an alteration inside him. He believed that it was his responsibility to be a part of the new destiny the rebels were pushing for. He felt connected; and he told himself that he had to tell the story of what DK's original people deserved, as opposed to the nothingness that the state had offered them. He shared with Gurnaam in detail all that he had seen. Gurnaam heard him in his quiet manner, asking him questions in between.

In the years to come, Neel made numerous journeys, travelling to guerrilla zones, getting acquainted with the leaders of the movement. He would take overnight buses from different cities, to towns and villages where his contact with the rebels would be established. He was now trained in the art of carrying only a small bag. Most days, he would have to be on the move, and he did not want the guerrillas lugging the weight of his belongings. The method of contact, each time he visited, remained the same, with minor changes. In one town, he was told to stand outside a temple with a flask. Somebody would come; the journey would begin. And he'd be in. There'd be new faces and old. He would stay for weeks, talking to guerrillas, trying to understand their motives, their inner lives. It was difficult to get into their heads. They were not articulate; they would take their time opening up. There was also the barrier of language. Since they did not have grand notions of themselves, they downplayed events or chose silence.

One evening, Neel had a long conversation with a woman. She was tender and shy and looked at him in an almost erotic way, fascinated by this outsider. The next morning, she was away, taking part in an ambush. In a video of that ambush, used later by the guerrillas for training purposes, Neel was shocked to see her killing injured paramilitary soldiers with a knife, and afterwards, removing their shoes, bulletproof jackets and radio sets. She had done this with the kind of impassiveness he had seen Adivasis displaying while burying their dead. The leaders, who would have read Fanon like him, placed themselves in the middle of everything, and listened to the radio under a nebulous sky; they believed that there would be a chair for them in history's tent, and in DK, a memorial painted in their memory with cheap red paint. The earthen lamp, like the one Neel had seen outside Sukhi Kaamrade's memorial, would, after some time, stay unlit. But that wouldn't matter.

M was always on the move; but so was he for his work, and a great friendship was formed between them. She was hungry for ideas, for making sense of the world beyond the guerrilla zone. Under starlit skies, next to angry rivers, Neel and she ended up spending several nights in discussion on subjects of common interest. Neel was bemused by her interest in mathematics. It was something close to his heart. The purity offered by some of its core components and the clarity it brought to the complexities of the larger universe were, for Neel, akin to the lucidity with which he envisioned home. He was excited to share with her the challenges inherent in mathematical puzzles; he described to her the pen scene in a movie on John Nash's life, and he told her about Alexander Grothendieck.

On a trip, three years later, he found himself in a camp, as usual under M's charge. He had to leave the next day, but due to some complications, which M did not share with him, the comrades could not escort him to the nearest road. Resigned, he waited in the camp. At one point, M was passing him by and he called out to her.

'Give me something to read. One of your manuals or anything,' he said.

M laughed. It was rare. 'You would be very happy to meet someone. I hope someday you get a chance,' she said.

'Who?'

She looked at him. 'My sister,' she said.

M had shared for the first time that she had a sister who was also in the 'party'.

'She works in a platoon in another area,' she added. She was a voracious reader, M said of her sister. But it was not possible to get many books in the zone. She said Gurnaam and others always brought some when they visited. 'But she finishes a book a day,' she said, smiling.

Three days later, M got a green signal and he was escorted out.

Neel got a chance to meet M again a year later when he was back in her area in DK. He was not sure if he would get to meet her sister; nevertheless, he carried a few books for her. At least M could send these to her.

That whole night, it had been raining. Like the guerrillas, he woke up around sunrise. He came out of his tarpaulin dwelling. Many of the camp inmates were not there—Neel thought they must be somewhere performing their military drills. The rain had cleaned the landscape. Somewhere, a bird was going mad with what felt to him like joy. His back was sore because of sleeping on the ground. Also, because of it, a cold dampness permeated through his body. He tried a few stretches and then walked towards the kitchen area. Luckily, the comrades were preparing tea in a battered utensil whose exterior was completely black with soot from the wood fire. They offered him a steel mugful of tea, loaded with sugar. Here, in these hard surroundings, sugar felt like nothing less than gaiety.

From the other end of the clearing, he saw a girl appearing with a small party. She was wearing canvas shoes without laces and had a rifle slung over her shoulder like M, who was not there at that moment. As Neel watched, a few young girls among the rebels rushed towards her. She hugged them and squealed like a schoolgirl.

Just then, M arrived.

It was touching to see this girl and M walk towards one another in a controlled manner. They stood face-to-face, arms on each other's shoulders. Their heads touched. They stayed like that for a moment, as if speaking through a secret, personal Morse code.

In a trance of sorts, Neel walked towards them. But the girl took no note of this stranger; perhaps, she had already been made aware of his distant presence. She removed her rucksack and took out a packet of sweets—there was a picture of a bespectacled man on it (which Neel later came to know was associated with a famous shop in Hyderabad; the bespectacled man was the owner, and his face was used as an emblem by the shop). The packet was from their past life, Neel thought, of which he had no clue.

'Neel,' said M, 'she is my sister, Gurupriya.'

Gurupriya raised her fist in greeting and said, 'Comrade, please tell me you have got books.'

Neel smiled. 'Maybe,' he said. As he took out books from his rucksack, Gurupriya almost snatched them from his hands. She was overjoyed to see Steinbeck's *The Grapes of Wrath* among them. 'There was a programme on the BBC about it once. I so wanted to read it,' she said.

'God wanted you to read this,' Neel said.

'We do not believe in god, Comrade,' she said.

'Well, I do. So, I'd like to attribute this little miracle to her,' Neel said.

'Okay, okay.' She laughed.

She spoke so differently from M, Neel thought. She could have been a recent pass-out from a fancy college. Unlike M, who kept her hair short, Gurupriya had long hair, its texture having gone rough in the forest.

As she kept flitting from tent to tent in the camp, Neel could not help but notice that she had an openness to her, a zest, which was more than just revolutionary spirit. In the evening, as several guerrillas went to a clearing in the forest for their military drills, Gurupriya stayed back, tutoring a class of young men and women, all of whom, Neel could see, were new recruits. He did not go into that tent, but from a distance he could see that the young Adivasis were totally engrossed.

He took out a cigarette and walked towards the other side of the gathering, constantly searching the ground. The other night, the guerrillas had found a venomous snake here that had to be killed. On a bent bough, a woman sat uncomfortably, and in front of her stood one of the young girls who had rushed earlier towards Gurupriya upon her arrival. She had recently joined the guerrillas, and the woman sitting on the bough was her mother, who had come to see her from a village about five miles away. They exchanged a few words, after which there was silence. Neel felt the quiet deeply and began thinking about its meanings.

'The deepest love is felt in silences, Comrade.'

He turned to see Gurupriya.

'I am wondering how often she gets to see her child.'

'Not very often, Comrade.'

'She may even die.'

'Yes.'

'Then what is the point of all this?'

'The point of all this is dignity, the right to life—a decent life—which has been denied to the poor.'

'For which she may lose her life?'

'For which all of us here in our ill-fitted uniforms are willing to die.'

'Is it worth it?'

She smiled. 'You city people, always measuring and calculating the worth of things.'

'Oh, come on ...'

'The right to life with dignity is not a thing, my friend. You cannot put a price to it.'

Neel did not want this to escalate. From his conversations with M and other leaders, he knew that committed members had immense belief in what they did. He had strong disagreements with some of their methods. But he had to respect their faith.

He tried to make light of things. 'Oh, so from Comrade, I have become "my friend". I am not sure if that is a promotion or a demotion.'

'For us, Comrade is the highest form of friendship. Comrade is saathi. The co-traveller. Far more revered than an ordinary friend, who may choose to take a different path.'

'So, I am demoted?'

She laughed and pushed her gun towards him.

'You'll have to earn it now.'

He took the weapon from her. Before this, he had never held a gun in his hands. Suddenly, he felt light-headed; he felt a power that he realized in an instant he was incapable of handling. He returned it to her without a word. She slung it upside down on her shoulder, as they all did with automatic weapons.

They were on the border of two states, in the contiguous guerrilla zone. The river next to their camp got flooded in the monsoons, its water brown and angry, carrying with it trees and big branches. 'This will take you straight to the crocodiles in the Indravati,' Gurupriya laughed as she said it.

Neel knew that the two sisters had no idea about his history. There never had been time, or occasion, to tell M. And Gurupriya, he had just met. In the pragmatic, cold world of guns, a softness of heart and body was undesirable. They sat quietly, enveloped by a sense of place and a sense of history he could not articulate.

Just then, M joined them. She had with her a handwritten note that Gurupriya had brought along with her—it was a message from a commander about something which they didn't wish to share with him. 'It's a biscuit,' M said. In their world, a letter—always a letter, since they never used any other mode of communication—was a biscuit. He realized that the two sisters did not have many opportunities to meet; the work in the guerrilla zone was regimented in that sense. At one point, another biscuit arrived. The two sisters quickly got up and asked Neel to return to his tent.

Neel had been with them for two weeks, when he came down with a strange fever. There were no chills, so malaria was ruled out. In a day, the fever rose so much that he became delirious. From the edge of consciousness, he could hear the comrades debating whether they should evacuate him. It would take three days of walking and carrying him on a makeshift stretcher to reach a treatment centre. But he suddenly got enough strength to put his hand on Gurupriya's wrist and squeeze it. She stopped in the middle of saying something; everyone became quiet. He didn't know what was happening, but they understood. They let him be.

At night, Gurupriya would come to check his fever. Others would come and go, too. When there was no one but her, she would sometimes keep her hand over his forehead and let it stay there for a few minutes.

A day after he had squeezed her wrist, Neel opened his eyes and saw a man peering over. It took a moment to recognize him. 'Doctor!' he mumbled.

'Hello. *Kee rola paaya hai*,' he smiled and said in Punjabi—what a cacophony have you created!

Neel noticed that he had developed a little paunch. He was carrying a rucksack full of medicines. He conducted some blood tests right there and gave him some pills. It took three more days; the fever finally came down. However, it left him enfeebled.

Ten more days passed. On the day he had to leave, the guerrillas stood in two neat columns, facing each other, and sang a farewell song, with the hope that they would meet again. M and Gurupriya were in opposite rows, facing each other, their fists held up in farewell, just like everyone else.

Neel had a Swiss knife in his bag. He had, in the last two decades, collected so many knives and paper cutters. For him, these were symbolic of cutting the belly of destiny's whale, of fighting back, of resisting irresolution. He had a strong urge to give it to Gurupriya, but he held himself back. It could be inappropriate in front of the entire group of rebels.

A day later, as he sat in a bus that would take him to the nearest town, he closed his eyes and imagined Gurupriya's hand over his blazing forehead.

*

Now, Gurupriya has turned up—ten years after he had first met her. She is standing next to the amaltas that Adaa and he had planted. He is relieved to see her. It is futile to ask how she made her way to his place.

'Listen, I want to tell you something before I go up. I need to lie low for a few days. We have friends here, but they could be under surveillance.' At this moment, she looks over his shoulder. 'I don't want to put you at risk. I cannot go anywhere else, but I will totally understand ...'

This time, he puts his hand over her mouth. Her shoulders, Neel sees, relax immediately. He takes her rucksack, and she silently follows him up two flights of stairs.

She sleeps for a full day and night once he shows her into the guest room. To Father, he says she is a social activist. Father is really surprised to see her sleeping so much and insists that Neel wake her up so that she can eat. For his sake, Neel slowly opens her door a few times, hoping she will stir. But she is in deep sleep. Only once does he see her face contort; she utters, 'Amma.' He knows what this means—she is missing the one who gave birth to her.

When she wakes up, she is apologetic. She has walked days to come out of the guerrilla zone. At one point, in the dead of the night, she had spotted floodlights on top of a hillock, which could only mean that state forces had occupied the highest point. She crawled for hours to pass undetected. It was a miracle that the forces were not in possession of night vision devices. Or maybe they were tired, too. The crawling induced severe backache and, more than that, a kind of fatigue she felt unable to shrug off.

She had escaped from an attack on the camp. Someone had given the rebels away, most likely an informer. Several leaders had died. The young woman he had seen years ago, standing in silence as her mother waited on that bough, had died too.

Neel knows what this means. The attack will have repercussions. Many more will be killed, including innocent villagers. If someone discovers Gurupriya's presence in his house, the reprisal will be brutal; he could go to jail for providing her shelter.

But as Neel looks at her, the consequences do not seem to matter. He feels deep affection for this girl.

On the third day, as he enters home, he hears Father's laughter. He cannot believe it. In his parents' room, there she is, mimicking Neel's posture, the way he frowns while speaking, how he gets up from the sofa, the way he grunts after losing patience and how it shows in his fidgety gestures. From her bed, Mother, who cannot speak or move, but whose senses are intact, is chuckling as well.

Gurupriya goes away to make tea; she says the house help must get some rest from her work. 'She is a good girl,' Father says. He doesn't say more, but Neel knows that he is trying to tell him something significant, that he wishes to attribute a special meaning to her stay.

How does Neel tell him that she is fighting for a different world—a world he will have no problem with, but a world that is hard to imagine? How does he tell him that her presence here could invite a knock and devastating repercussions?

'Comrade,' he says as he approaches the guest room—she's here after making tea. She looks up from the book she has picked off his shelf. She senses something in his voice. She waits.

'Why don't you come here?' he asks.

'What do you mean?'

'I mean ... come here, live here, work here. Find a job, marry, have children, send them to school. They will call you Amma.'

She doesn't say anything; the fingers that were running over the page she was reading stop cold. It is late evening; by the light of the table lamp, he can see the colour of her face changing. He can see the scars on her arms, her fingers probably carry cuts.

'I will leave tomorrow,' she says. That is her answer.

At night, he dreams of her corpse floating in the river. He has a strong feeling that she will get caught in a snare.

The next morning, at 4.30 a.m., she is at his door. She is leaving. 'It's best that I go on my own and that you know nothing about it till you hear from me again.' She pauses. 'Fingers crossed.' She smiles. 'Don't you guys like to say that?'

'I am not "you guys", Gurupriya. I am someone who sits cross-legged and prays to god that you emerge unscathed.'

This revelation moves her. Neel thinks that her eyes are glistening all of a sudden with emotion. But very quickly, she takes control. She smiles, takes two steps, and hugs Neel.

He still harbours some dreams—of Gurupriya's 2 BHK in the city, of her driving lessons, of her family, of her Amma who'll come and help during pregnancy.

It is her welfare, her safety, her freedom, her dignity that concerns him; he wants to push away the dread that she will end up on a blue tarpaulin sheet in a police photograph.

Gurupriya won't change course. She is in thrall to the idea of a revolution, of a vision that she believes will be the precursor to a good life, of a communist Narnia. She is in thrall to a home that will keep eluding her, just as it eludes him. This much he knows. He wishes it weren't the case.

'Wait,' he says. He goes to his drawer and takes out the Swiss knife he was supposed to have given her a long time ago. It has a red body. 'Just keep it with you at all times,' he says. This is the only talisman he can offer her, a talisman that he prays will keep her alive.

'Goodbye, saathi,' she says.

He watches her walk towards the main road, past the amaltas tree that looks laden in gold. To her, you cannot even say: drop me a message when you reach.

He goes to the guest room and takes in its emptiness. Gurupriya's body needed rest for five years, not five days. She could have stayed back, she could have taken a sabbatical from the revolution. Neither he nor she needed to define this as anything more than rest and recuperation. There'd be enough books here to last her five years. She could have taken them with her to her own apartment. Or read them here whenever she desired.

Come and go as you please, he says to her in his head.

The city needs a revolution, too, Comrade, he hears her reply.

But it won't happen now. One hotelier told Neel why he kept a big TV in his staff quarters. His employees worked hard, for twelve to fourteen hours, after which they went to the quarters, ate food in front of the TV and fell asleep. The TV gave them no opportunity to examine their lives.

How do you wake them up—a people who are used to soporific entertainment?

Gurupriya has neatly folded the light duvet she used to cover herself with. She has left no signs of her stay except for the fragrance of coconut oil. She used the fan, but never the air conditioner. This is the only luxury she accorded herself.

Father is disappointed when he learns of her departure. He is not expressive. Neel knows he will never talk about her again. Father's way of dealing with uncertainty is to reject the possibility that anything is certain. In a sense, he will always be more learned than Neel.

*

After Gurupriya's departure, the fatigue he had felt in that circuit house in the cut-off area became even sharper. A deep sense of futility pervaded him. He realized that what he had told Gurupriya—to stop, to build roots—he had to tell himself, too. He needed to find a way of disentangling himself from his aporia.

Another realization came with this—that he wanted more time to himself; that he desired slowness.

Some assignments had been offered, and he understood that he was getting them because no one else could work in the adverse conditions he had willed himself to get used to. Yet, he had also reached a stage in life where he had gathered enough of those experiences that Gurnaam had, long ago, told him he required.

The time had come to make sense of these experiences within a broader philosophical framework. He wanted to explore Ungrund, its meanings beyond himself, to see what Western philosophy had to offer *his* world. He longed to understand 'both the fallibility and the endurance of love'—the central preoccupation in Gillian Rose's *Love's Work*.

As he began to devote time to these pursuits and let go of other engagements (or, at least, minimize them), he wasn't aware that a storm was about to hit his body. That as it blew past, it would leave him behind, frozen, prone, on the summit of love.

When that happened, he imagined his body being used for direction—the way the frozen bodies of mountaineers on the Everest are made use of: 'Oh, turn left from that Tabard man.'

PART TWO
ENTROPY

He has been invited to a seminar in the south. He has barely travelled here, beyond the territories which are part of DK. He decides to make this a longer trip. The seminar organizers put him in touch with a travel agency. A driver, who speaks English and who knows the region well, is assigned to him.

It's a pilgrimage, he tells himself. A pilgrimage means that the idea of a god has been evoked.

He hasn't been to a temple in years. But, as he reaches Srirangam the next day, he finds himself in a long queue, along with throngs of people. As they approach the sanctorum, some of them utter, 'Ranga, Ranga,' with tears rolling down their cheeks. Like them, he is moved at the sight of Lord Vishnu in recline; he's resting on the serpent.

The next stop is Thanjavur, to visit the Brihadeeswara Temple. It is a world unlike the one he lives in. Sometimes he attributes what he witnesses to the selective vision—mostly rosy—of a pilgrim. That tint apart, he feels continuity, as if his heart, which started beating in his chest just over forty years ago, had been ticking elsewhere for a millennium.

This trip has been triggered by a particular image, by a picture shot by an artist called Santu Brahma. In the outer compound of Thillai Nataraja Temple, a woman—her back towards the photographer, in a withered sari, palms raised upwards—is in what looks like a deep conversation with the goddess. There is one word Neel associates with the image, the sound of which stays with him—kovil, which in Tamil means residence of a god, or, simply put, a temple. For him, in his travels, the kovil becomes part of a bigger vision, a beautiful aesthetic experience, as if he had come a step closer to Leibniz's paradise.

Strangely, he also becomes aware of what love demands; of what Rilke meant when he said that loving is 'work, day labor … day labor; God knows there is no other word for it.' It asks for toil; it asks you to find magic beyond the days of courtship, beyond the peacock dance; it asks that you believe in it, like the daily rising of the sun, and that you return to the wooden table. He knows of his fatigue, his exhaustion with the world around him. But the wooden table will not let go of its hold on him.

In the last leg of the journey, he finally reaches Tiruvannamalai, to spend a few days at the Sri Ramanasramam. His room is inside the ashram premises, in front of a huge banyan tree. A small gate by its side leads to a flight of stairs, to a cave where the seer meditated in his early days.

His room has a basic cot, a table and a chair. In the small bathroom, there is a bucket and a mug, and a rope to hang clothes on. The ashram serves two meals a day. He eats with other ashram inmates, sitting cross-legged on the floor, surrounded by pictures of devotees who arrived in the ashram at some point and could never leave. The food is delicious and filling. He wakes up early, very early, and sits in a corner of the compound; he barely speaks to others, most of whom also prefer it that way.

Initially, he finds it difficult. But sooner than he expects, he becomes comfortable. Every second day, he circumambulates the Arunachala mountain, by the foothills of which the ashram is built. Several times, he climbs up and sits on a flat rock, looking at the old temple below. When the time comes, he finds himself reluctant to leave.

It is raining furiously. The day of his departure for Chennai has been set, from where he'll take a flight to Delhi. He says goodbye to a few ashram inmates and drags his suitcase along the path outside, where foreigners who live on the premises for an extended period park their scooters. He is envious of them; their freedom is much more nuanced than his can ever be. He is bound by strange, unsaid doctrines of duty.

The cab moves along the beautiful road leading to Chennai, made further alluring by the lashing rain. By night, he will be back to a strange restlessness.

It is still raining when the cab drops him at the Chennai airport. After the security check, as he slips his leather belt through the loops of his jeans, a young woman appears in front of him.

'Hi,' she says.

'Hi.'

'If you are not in a hurry, can we talk for a few minutes? Also … will you sign my copy?' She produces his last book from her handbag.

*

That day at the airport, she mostly speaks to him about his work. He does not like talking about it.

Back in the day, when he'd return from the forest, he couldn't stop speaking of his experiences—of the newness of his encounters; of the starkness of everything, compared to what he had seen so far. It had left him confounded. But people did not get the scale of it. It was difficult to imagine that landscape.

As Neel and the young woman continue speaking, walking by the flickering gate numbers, past the bottles of perfumes and leather bags, and the display shelves of bookshops where, on the face of it, Neel gets the impression that the bestseller list has not changed in years, he takes a deep breath, and, with it, a proper look at the woman beside him. He suddenly feels as if they have just arrived together at the airport and are now trying to orient themselves.

She speaks in an English with a texture that is so different from his; she does not speak hurriedly, but at a pace which is faster and more convivial than his own measured tone.

'I saw you enter through the main gate and followed you. I hesitated for a long time before I finally said to myself that the worst that could happen was that you wouldn't talk to me,' she says.

'Why? Do I look so unapproachable?'

'Well, not unapproachable, really.' She stops, and he stops, and they turn towards each other. He can feel a trolley coming to a halt behind them, and he moves closer to her to give way.

'You have this brooding intensity,' she says, this time slowly.

He doesn't respond. She moves on from that statement. Her name is Aarani, she says, and she lives in Mumbai. She had come to Chennai to meet her grandfather who lives alone—in an old house by the sea, she tells him.

'I was very moved by your Dhondu essay,' she says.

It was something he had written with measured but forceful anger, about how far journalism had landed from the human concerns it was meant to foreground. In a border village, there had been a fire in an ordinance depot, causing shells and missiles to rain down on the modest houses in the vicinity; some of them had been destroyed completely. A television journalist he knew had gone there to cover it. What is your name, he asked a man whose house smouldered behind him. The man was weeping and was only able to tell his name in fits and starts. 'Dho ... n ... du,' he sobbed. 'What?' the journalist asked. 'Dho ... ndu,' the man wailed. By this time, a strange kind of vileness had crept into the journalist's heart. He had heard the name, but he had travelled some distance; he believed he deserved a little fun.

'What ... I cannot hear you,' he said.

'Dhondu, sir, Dhondu.' The man could not stop weeping. This went on for a long, long time.

The world is largely that journalist, Neel had told himself.

And now, this woman in front of him seems to know it, too.

'What does your name mean?' Neel asks her.

'Oh, I was named after a town called Arni; my grandfather comes from there. It is famous for its silk saris.'

There are two streams that run in a parallel manner in Neel's head. One, that there is a possibility that he will be translucently clear to her. He also thinks that she is awash with a resplendence that is stirring solid desire in him. As they sit next to each other, he tries hard not to look at her in a way that will give away the feeling she has produced in him. She keeps talking, continuing to mention things from his work, to convey to him, he thinks, how thoroughly she has combed through his writings.

Other details emerge. She has a master's in art history from UCL and works for an art magazine. He is often wrong about such things, but she appears to be someone in her late twenties.

'Do you want a drink?' she asks.

Before he can answer, she looks at her watch. 'Sorry, I don't think I have the time; boarding will start any time.' Then she adds: 'Is it okay if I took your phone number?'

He dictates it to her. 'Can I have yours?' He punches the number into his phone.

'Oh, I forgot,' she says and points to his book; it hasn't been signed yet. He cannot think of anything clever to write. So, he scribbles his name. She says goodbye and turns.

A panic sets in his heart. What if the phone develops a fault and all the numbers are erased? What if he loses it?

He takes out his notebook and writes down her number. Then he draws a fence around it, as he does around vital pieces of information.

Suddenly, he looks up and finds her standing in front of him with her trolley bag. (God, has she noticed him writing down her number? The fence?)

'You know what, it is okay, I can catch the next one,' she says.

The night is magical. They sit at the farthest table in the airport bar, drinking overpriced whisky. Their flights have long departed; he has lost all sense of the world around him. He is torn between listening to her and looking at her—and it sounds easy but is a most difficult thing to do.

Suddenly, both these urges are gone. Suddenly, he has this vision of them together in the kovil: she walks a little ahead of him in the temple courtyard, and he is intoxicated by the fragrance of jasmines in her hair, and the caretaker of the temple elephant greets her in Tamil, and she turns around to see if he is following her and then hands over to him the little plate with camphor and an assortment of flowers and an earthen lamp, and adjusts her sari.

As his mind returns to the semi-darkness of that corner in the bar, Aarani is still talking. She has questions about his travels to the guerrilla zone in DK, about his writing habits, about Kashmir. He answers them, even as he hears the bell around the elephant's neck, and though he tries, he cannot find any questions to ask her. In response to his answers, she asks more questions, as if she wanted to immerse herself in the cold plunge that is his life. He wants to protect her from the violence he has witnessed, from the images of dying men holding their entrails, from the pictures of torsos that have landed on high-tension wires, from the fear in the eyes of people who know there is no way out. So, he hands over to her a defanged version of the narrative-snake.

Time is time, and it passes quickly. It is almost dawn, and they must part ways to take their respective rescheduled flights. Neel resists the idea.

He wants to make a hoax bomb call to the airlines, as jilted lovers sometimes do. He wants to hold this woman and say, don't go; I was wrong; I don't want to live in an ashram. He wants to follow her to the coast she is travelling to—so, as the sun comes up, they can watch fishermen in their little boats together.

I want to live with you, in a house with a long wooden table.

He walks her to her gate.

'Do you think we will remain in touch?' she asks.

'I would like to,' he says.

Almost on cue, they both come closer and lightly embrace. He turns towards his gate. Once, he glances back. From her chair, she is looking at him.

As he boards his flight, he realizes that he has absolutely no recollection about the travellers at the other tables in the bar. He thinks of sending her a message, but decides against it. He puts his phone on airplane mode.

There is a beautiful sun out in Delhi as the flight begins to descend. The rays fall on his face in a frenzy when the plane takes a turn. He closes his eyes and it feels as though the light is bleaching his dread. The warmth of wellbeing permeates his body. Is this a renewal of the soul or is it simply nature's response to that ancient call for furthering the species, bearing children?

He wants to jump out of the plane, run across the terminal and sit in the sun in some café in Rome, eat a quiche and drink cups of coffee, as water gurgles out of the Trevi Fountain.

The plane lands, and as it is taxiing towards the gate, he switches on his phone. 'You should come to Bombay,' a message from her reads.

How do you fall in love? When you say you love someone, what does it signify?

For him, love has two components. One is the miraculous phenomenon through which all the beauty of the world converges on the face of the beloved. There may be other faces he also finds beautiful, but here, in the person he is drawn to, everything is in place—the face is the garden of paradise, and it is only with this person that a physical (external) garden of paradise—what home really feels like to him—can be built. The beloved is the one who has the power to prevent dread from returning after everyone has left the party. It is the assurance of her, the warmth of her body, that makes the tundra of the universe bearable. It is her face for which he feels like growing flowers. It is this person for whom—if she is the first to die—he will put a gun in his mouth and blow his brains out. She's the one he can hold a missal for, as she struggles with a hymn; for whom all the terms of endearment known to mankind fall short, so he has to invent an entirely new language; before whom he can iron out his thoughts while smoking a cigarette on a cold, dark night. It is her mannerisms he will learn and unknowingly adopt, till all the people, everywhere, start saying: 'Oh, look at them! They are like brother and sister!'

His love is also anchored deeply in friendship, in extraordinary loyalty. He sometimes imagines himself as having been raised in an orphanage, where he meets a girl, an orphan like him, and their bond becomes strong within the difficult environs of the institution. There are two more orphans like them, another boy and a girl. The four become close. When they are older, he marries the girl; the other boy marries the other girl. They inhabit one house and make a covenant that they will always be together. They may face the outside world separately, but once they are within this home they have built, they are a unit. Nobody else will matter even a fraction of what they mean to one another. They drink coffee together; they know each other's tics and likes and dislikes; they have a single playlist; they cook as one and take common trips. They are inseparable.

Given the sharpness of his idea of home and of love, it has been difficult for Neel to respond to any gesture that suggests an interest in him. Or to convey his interest in someone. Because in front of the minutiae he has conjured up, the universe largely looks imprecise. But now, a human pickaxe in her late twenties (he was right, she's twenty-nine!), wearing a red tee and ice-blue jeans and a pair of sneakers, has ripped through the rink of his heart.

*

And there she is, there they are.

A week later, he is in Mumbai to meet her.

They have decided to meet at a bar, one among many in a compound that previously served as a textile processing unit. He takes a cab from his hotel and reaches there a little early. It is June and it is always raining. It is beginning to get dark. On the other side of the street, he sees her walk towards the bar and come to a halt. She is wearing a dress. He takes a moment to look at her. His first instinct is that he needs to protect her at all costs.

He crosses the road.

'Hello,' he says.

He does not remember what else they say to each other in that moment. They enter the bar and sit by a huge glass window. He notices that she has a big gash on her leg. 'I wanted you to see this,' she says. It is an injury from a recent trek in the Himalayas. He realizes later that it is her thing—to put everything on the table. The display of the gash is part of that ethic—a remnant of her past that he has to make peace with.

At one point, a waiter who knows her brings them a complimentary snack. Later, on her recommendation, Neel tries a cocktail that she says the sommelier makes well.

It is drizzling as they come out; the droplets of rain stick to their clothes like powder. The lights, the little pockets of darkness, and the shrieks of delight coming from intoxicated patrons—all of these make him feel as if he is at a fair. The scene registers in his mind as an ideogram, rounded out with a Ferris wheel. She subtly holds his hand as they take a stroll, and the ideogram turns musical—he swears he can hear an accordion.

They take a cab back to his hotel. The old elevator that takes them up reminds him of the one in the Yale building. Annie flashes through his mind—but he pushes away that thought.

Inside the room, he kisses her, and she raises herself on her toes and kisses him back. He kisses her again, this time more intensely. She looks at him with an expression he can only describe as 'unfathomableness'.

'You know, you have a sorrow nerve,' she says.

'I thought I had a brooding intensity.'

'You have. The sorrow nerve is its jewel.'

Later, he notices it, a tiny vein that makes its appearance below his left eye. He can list all the experiences that have led to its formation. But with her, such things hardly matter.

The next evening, he is off to meet her again. It shocks him that one night has changed him so much. His senses are heightened and he begins to pay attention to things. By the sea, lovers have stopped their bikes and they stand in a row, in twos, to share moments of tenderness. They do not notice him, but he wants to wave at them. He is in love. *I adore this girl, this woman, who tiptoes to kiss me.* The Dooley Wilson song plays in his head, and he sees decanters and leisurely Sundays and March ice creams.

They get into a pattern quickly.

She comes every morning to his hotel room, after her aerobics class. He is by the window, on the chair, when she enters. She sits on his lap, putting her arms around his neck. Her heart beats fast. There is a film of sweat on her body. Her hair is frizzy. He is filled with vitality, a life force that Nietzsche called 'Rausch'. She goes back home, and then to her office, from where she messages him all day.

In the evening, they meet at this bar or that. He feels a surge of love for her, and this love, to his mind, is a lifetime commitment to her welfare, to being her best friend, to watching her become what Aristotle called a 'second self'.

*

The next few days, he is so happy that he disbelieves the quantum of it.

Something else happens that is extraordinary. In Aarani's presence, he is very sleepy. It is a different sleep, a dreamless sleep, like one induced by anaesthesia. He is unable to tell how long he is gone. He knows this is because, with her, his usual fight-or-flight responses are put to rest and the parasympathetic nervous system takes over. It may sound like a contradiction, but he is also fully awake (or active—which Erich Fromm said was an indispensable condition for the practice of love). In other words, both his comatose and awake selves have undergone a tremendous change. He wants to write—a book, a film, a poem.

Words come to him like snowflakes.

His neurons are luminous like fireflies.

While she is away at office by day, he finishes work meetings. A film-maker asks him to write a web series based on his work in Maoist areas. Such prompting would not have excited him in the past, but now there is Aarani. He calls her immediately and tells her about the meeting. The promise of a home with her has stirred in him a deep desire to live.

Quite simply, he wants to give all his love to her. He feels inside himself an immense capacity to cherish her. He's not unlike a hydroelectric plant, whose turbines have received water from a mighty river.

That tiny hotel room: home, home, home.

On the hotel's letter pad, Aarani creates for him a to-do list:

Write

Stay off poison (the poison of bitterness—she feels he carries it inside)

Meet people

Keep yourself busy
Love me

His last day in Mumbai is a Sunday. She goes home in the afternoon, promising to return in an hour or so. It is raining heavily, and he has put on a Kishori Amonkar playlist. Beyond the glass window, for days a bulldozer hasn't stopped churning the earth; the mud reveals some ancient colour that he imagines flows from the jugular vein of the Ashvamedha horse. Over the sound of the rain lashing against the glass window, Amonkar's voice triumphs: *Ab ke mile to bicchuda na jaaye, sahela re*.

Aarani opens the door, and he gets up and kisses her, and keeps her dripping umbrella in the bathtub, and immediately wolfs down all the feasts of love she has to offer. Afterwards, as they watch curtains of rain falling in criss-crossing patterns, she looks at him and says, 'I want a home with you.'

At that moment, he forgets that he has a sorrow nerve; he forgets how an old ascetic had told his father that he would have to keep walking—paed raah—as if mythical hunters were after him.

She is carrying with her a beautiful dress that she says she will wear that night. As she gets into the shower, he takes out the iron and the board from the closet. The iron glides over the dress, and he can smell her perfume on it. She comes out, sees him smelling it and says she could not clean it as it needed to be hand-washed. On the hotel notepad, with a hotel pencil, then, he writes her a note: *I promise to wash one thousand pieces of clothing of the bearer of this note, with the possibility of a lifelong extension*. He signs it.

They go to Colaba, to Café Mondegar, and sit under a poster that says, 'I hear dead people and they're still the best.' From their conversation, a little emerges of her life. She is an only child who has never felt affection coming from her father. She has struggled with her mental health; she has been seeing a therapist for what she can best describe as mood swings.

He thinks: we are both looking for the same thing, a soulmate with whom we can gang up against the world; we are both committed to what Hegel called 'becoming one organ in a living whole'. She wants me to be by her side, on her side, against the entire universe.

He wants her as well, on his side, even if he is on the wrong side. They will have to drag each other away from the larger world's effluvium. It is something Barthes wrote about in *A Lover's Discourse*. Someone he refers to as X once told him that 'love had protected him against worldliness: coteries, ambitions, advancements, interferences, alliances, secessions, roles, powers ...'

But then, Neel has another thought. He fears that Aarani is young, and he is now a middle-aged man who is preoccupied with too many things, has too much history.

'I feel old in my bones,' he tells her.

That night, after she has returned home, she sends him a text message—she's paraphrasing a line from a Leonard Cohen song: 'You are my snowman with second-hand physique.'

*

Once he is back in Delhi, he feels a pain in his heart because of her absence.

They call each other every day. She is usually in a cab back home when she calls; or she is headed to a bar to meet her friends. He is not averse to drinking, but he notices that she drinks a lot. He says he misses her touch, the intimacy, the spooning, the sound of her voice that has retained something of her southern roots, despite the fact that she has grown up in Mumbai.

He begins writing, filled with a potency he has not known before. His step is light, and it feels as though some demon has released his foot from his chest. The pain in his abdomen is also fading. He is lifting weights, his running becomes more agile. He is meeting people—new people—as he had promised Aaru. In Kim's café, he sits at his usual seat for hours, making life plans, creating imaginary Excel sheets of all that Aaru and he will do once they are together.

He has never seen a picture of her parents, and sometimes he wonders who between the two she resembles. She doesn't like to speak about them beyond the tiny details she has already offered, and he can see that there is no openness even with her mother. He imagines having a drink with her father; he imagines telling him about his travels. He imagines going to Aaru's kitchen and laughing with her mother, with whom he will share secrets; he imagines the mother going silent as Aaru enters, and Aaru rolling her eyes and saying, 'Ya, ya, complain about me, don't let me come in the way, I am just taking water from the fridge.'

His idea of love is inspired by all kinds of visions. But where do these originate from? He does not have a clue.

He wants to be in Aaru's room and play with the soft-toy elephant that rests on her bedside table; he wants to sit on the floor and see pictures of her childhood—the schoolgirl in pigtails and white canvas shoes, perhaps in a mock sari for a school performance.

But there is some part of her that he feels he has no access to. This inaccessibility appears at times like a sluice gate. Unexpectedly, a hidden self penetrates through her outward playfulness. Her face then assumes a strange pallor; her hair does not smell of fruity shampoo but of beer.

One day, he is in the library when he receives her call. He rushes out to answer it. From the other end, her voice emerges, and it sounds as if Aaru is drowning at high tide. 'I have achieved nothing in life; you are established, you are an acclaimed author,' she says.

Oh, Aarani. There are times when he thinks he overdoes it, giving too much of himself to people, sharing with them what has come to him with much difficulty and perseverance. But Aaru is not *people*, she is a piece of his heart. All his knowledge, all his insights are at her disposal. As in that Kipling poem, he is happy to make a heap of all his winnings. He is happy to toss it at her feet.

I will dig the earth and send tributaries of information to you. Do what you want with it. Write a book. Travel. Let me take you to a village in DK. Let me show you what happens to the heart when someone fires an AK-47. Let me lead the way to Ramanasramam. Will you wear a sari, become a part of the image I associate with a kovil? Can I tell you what it does to my mind, meditating on Philip K. Dick's comment on the cosmos; that it 'may in fact do nothing but think'? Can I recite a line from the Mahabharata that gives me goosebumps? Can I tell you about Simone Weil and her discovery of George Herbert's poem 'Love', and that I imagine her reciting it on a bed of dry straw in a farm in Avignon? Can I tell you about the life of Stanisława Przybyszewska, of whom I know through a Hilary Mantel lecture? What are we, if not stories? What is your story, Aaru? Tell me of things beyond your office or your immediate group of friends. Tell me what you imagine; tell me what you think.

In essence, Neel wonders what Aaru wants. At home, he stands in front of the bedroom closet, thinking of the kind of space she'll require for her things. She can have all she desires. The transition from Mumbai to Delhi will be difficult. He'd be glad to make the move instead of her. But he cannot ask his parents to shift home again—so many of their years have been spent in constant flux, fearing the tyranny of landlords—nor can he leave them alone here and go. He will try and make her life as comfortable as possible.

What is the smell she likes waking up to every morning? Filter coffee? Dosai? And what sounds?

Later, it strikes him that he has never had such conversations with her—of these small things that matter even more than the big ones. All that has gone in the imaginary Excel sheet is from him alone.

Love is continual interrogation, Milan Kundera wrote.

During his time with Aaru, there has been no interrogation—and its absence is perceived by Neel only later.

*

After a month, she flies to Delhi. He is happy that she is coming. He picks her up from the airport. She hugs him as soon as she sees him and they are unable to break the embrace. He has booked them into a hotel near his house. They check in and devour each other for a few hours.

In the evening, he takes her to a popular bar. He would have liked to go to a quieter place, but he knows she likes crowded pubs. There is a live band playing; he has to raise his voice significantly to speak, and he strains to hear her.

They return late at night and walk for a bit outside the hotel. He gets coffee from the hotel café and they sit on the pavement. Afterwards, they go to the room and make love. He is hungry for her. He falls into a deep sleep once more. He wakes up early. She is still asleep, her lipstick smudged across her cheek. He wants to give her all the happiness she can carry.

After an hour or so, she wakes up and looks at him and calls him to bed. She needs to be held, he knows it. He holds her and strokes her hair. Her body loosens and she drifts back to sleep. He keeps holding her that way.

At some point, she wakes up. 'I am hungry,' she says. They go down to the restaurant and eat the breakfast buffet.

'What do you want to do today?' he asks.

He takes her to Kim's café—he wants to make her familiar with the places that mean something to him. Aaru is wearing jeans and the same red tee she wore when they met first, and an uneven layer of lipstick. They have some more coffee and she keeps looking at the high-rise apartments all around. At some point, they have lunch, and later, drive to South Delhi. He takes her to a Caribbean bar. 'Some beer would be nice,' she says. He invites a friend, who is an art critic. Together, they laugh a lot about a recent political development.

His body cannot process so much alcohol. He feels droopy. They drive back to the hotel; it is close to midnight when they reach. He gets into the shower and changes into a pair of shorts. She is sitting in bed, watching a British soap. He lies down next to her.

It feels as if she is calling his name. He opens his eyes. He looks at her and realizes that he had dozed off. He can also see that she has switched off the TV—the remote is in her hands; it looks like a club that she might hit him with.

'I cannot believe that you slept off! I am leaving tomorrow and you just slept off,' she says.

'I thought you were watching TV, Aarani. And I did not mean to sleep. I just dozed off. I am sorry.'

'No ... you don't care.'

Suddenly, he feels angry. He loses control. At that moment, everything is lost. Later, he revisits the instant a million times. It could have been salvaged quite easily. She was having a mood swing. He could have apologized again and said, 'Let me hold you. I will not sleep the entire night. You sleep, I will hold you.'

But he does not do that. His anger has given rise to an exhaustion, followed by the same paralysis, the same stammering of action. He glares at her and turns to his side. That is it.

He can almost tell that she is in the same position. But he has crossed over. There is nothing he can do; there is nothing he is capable of doing. A peculiar drowsiness embraces him like a cloud. He is invisible. He goes underwater to the bottom of the ocean.

When he comes up, it is morning. But the paralysis stays. He can see that Aarani has been taken aback by his lack of response. He cannot break the spell. She looks at him from the corner of her eye, hoping that he will say something. But he does not. At some point, she mumbles that she is going down for breakfast. In hindsight, he believes that she said it hoping that he would volunteer to come along too. But he is no longer in charge; the ghoul possesses his soul. So, he stays immobile.

He is packing his bag when she returns from breakfast. They have at least three more hours to check out, and another three hours before she is to reach the airport. But time has become an ordeal for him now. He wants to be alone, locked up in his room. She looks at him and starts packing her bag, too. In fifteen minutes, they sit in the car. He doesn't know what to do, so he brings her back to Kim's café. She keeps looking at him, then at her coffee, which she does not touch. He finishes one cup, then another.

Suddenly, she cannot take it. She gets up. 'I think I will leave for the airport,' she says. He does not try stopping her. He calls the driver. She says she will go on her own. He pays no heed to her. The car appears in the driveway, he opens the door and she gets in. 'Drop her at the airport,' he tells the driver.

And just like that, she leaves in the car, five hours before she is supposed to be at the airport. He feels relieved to see that she is gone. The relief, he knows, is temporary, purely in response to the fact that the awkwardness has ended.

Now, a gorge has fallen open between them. All he must do is take a giant leap to cross it and be on the same side as her. But he cannot move an inch.

The next few months are a blur. He shuts himself in. It is a sort of immune response, something primal inside him trying to protect his body. Being out, not isolating himself, and yet not confronting things, can only create poison within his being. He already has too much of it. There is bitterness from the past; there is resentment, too, for his failure to achieve his ideal aesthetic. He had the wherewithal to achieve it, even without love in the mix. And yet, there have been impediments. Nobody understands it as well as he does.

A few days after her return, Aaru tries contacting him. Again and yet again. These attempts are typically made late at night, when she's returning home after a few drinks. He picks up her calls a few times in the early days. But no breakthrough seems possible. They do not talk about the night when things collapsed or about the morning after. He does not commit to lifting his share of the weight. He knows no thaumaturgy with which to untangle this knot.

Very quickly, he falls into a different way of life, which, in his heart, he knows is pastiche. He begins to pursue women who are bored of their married lives and want attention and sex. Sex is not hard for them to get, but in a world of constant distraction, where people are losing the ability to listen, an attentive fling is the new diamond. The women want this without rocking their boat. Their life—apart from the presence of boredom—is stable. They have children who have been diagnosed with ADHD by fancy therapists; and there are joint bank accounts and properties.

He keeps at it due to a spectacular lust that has risen inside him; that has taken over, serpent-like, so he loses control. He has turned into that farmer in the steamy video who wants 'breakfast' all the time. Physical strength rises within him, too, making him do things with weights that shock him. He could not get out of the loop of fifty-eight push-ups; now, suddenly, he is doing a hundred. He is the war elephant in Alexander's army; he is deathless, ageless and infallible.

He meets a radiologist at a party and takes her to bed. He sees a woman with a toddler in a supermarket, and a day later, he is fucking her. Another woman: he makes her sit at the edge of a bed in a hotel room overlooking the ruins of Delhi, and mutters things to her. Ten minutes later, she explodes, uttering a guttural 'damn you'. She is then unable to say anything; her pupils are dilated. To another woman he has known for years, he sends a message. She calls him home; he removes her clothes and pours Chilean wine on her in her bathtub.

His seed is spreading like a Rorschach inkblot.

*

After such licentiousness, he'd return frayed; he'd feel as if he had kept his brain in a microwave oven. It surprised him how light the women's faces turned at the end of each rendezvous.

Upon getting home with a heaviness in his heart, he'd get into a pattern of dreadful doomscrolling—of waking up at 2.10 a.m.; of reaching for his phone and watching Instagram reels; of finally slipping back into sleep. His reading went down drastically, and he forgot all about writing. He'd pick up a book, his eyes running through a line or two without absorbing anything, and then, he'd return to his cell phone, as though it were a welcoming bosom. He began to get dreams;

these were not terrifying, but bizarre, like a Dali painting, and the morning after weighed heavily on him.

A sign that he had withdrawn from an inner life was that he did not remember how he felt about Aarani. It was not a question of what. There was only love for her, and a desire—a physical desire—that made something alive inside him. Now that was gone. He felt estranged from a plan of action, from a way of telling her that he loved her and wanted her back.

The embrace of Aarani's memory became a blur. From the outside, he saw her on Instagram, drinking with two or three friends she hung out with, with accorded nicknames—it's what the young in Mumbai are wont to do. There were photos in which she sat cross-legged on some futon, a gypsy necklace against a sleeveless top. Or in which she stood in a dark alley with a plastic tumbler—which, he knew, meant that it was well past midnight, and the bars had closed, and people were abruptly being asked to leave; their drinks had been poured into plastic tumblers as takeaway.

Sometimes, he wondered if things would have been different between them had she considered—or even attempted—taking a leap over the pitch-fork static of her family. He began rummaging through his memories, unearthing conversations with her. There were small clues all over. She had rejected, vehemently, anything that could make her come close to confronting her own self. He understood this. The inside of a human being can be a frightful thing—like those ugly, monstrous creatures that oceanographers come across sometimes in the depths of the waters. He himself was wary of what he'd find inside himself if he chose to search for long. But, at least, he was not shutting out the possibility or getting away from it.

He also realized that he could not make Aarani to order—or hammer her into a version of herself that he'd find easy to live with. Would she, after that alteration, be the same person he fell in love with; whose breasts he had cupped delicately in his hands; who looked at him, sometimes, in a way that would make him want to simply die for her? This is when she came closest to her real self. Too often, though, that self got blocked.

He wanted badly to put his hand into whatever pit a part of her was lost in. But his own hands bled. A bleeding hand, he knew, would be of no help.

So, he stayed away.

Her phone calls kept coming in the same fashion. He'd wake up in the morning and find that she had tried calling at forty minutes past midnight. No matter the breakthrough they may have achieved, he had to admit that the relationship would not be sustainable. So, he sent her messages—text messages—when he knew she'd be sober. As expected, these were met with wry remarks and not something solid that he could turn into a scaffolding.

It was what it was. Ultimately, we are in charge of our individual cups of hemlock; no one can drink them on our behalf.

The phone calls decreased at first, then stopped altogether. He put a hold on his messages. He would meet her once after this. Then, a vast ocean would come in the way.

*

One afternoon, he is driving to Kim's café, when he receives a message from Joshua. Philip Roth has died at the age of eighty-five. They are going to bury him at the Bard College Cemetery, as per his wishes.

It is May, and in the summer heat, Neel stops near a park and gets in. On the bench, he sits next to a bunch of labourers, some of whom are laying down fibre-optic cables, while their kids play nearby in the dirt. He browses the web and reads through an overwhelming number of obituaries. Roth has chosen to be buried next to the spot reserved for his friend, Norman Manea; he has forbidden all Jewish rituals.

Neel watches the burial on TV later. The gravesite is near a tree (a pine tree, he later comes to know), and he can hear the faint sound of vehicles passing along Route 9G outside. Manea reads an excerpt from Roth's *The Dying Animal*. The camera pans to the left, and it suddenly feels as if Neel has been hit. A little away from an elderly man, Annie stands by herself, her knees clenched.

'Don't pan away, don't pan away,' he mutters, as if the camera person can hear him. The camera shifts back to Manea, and Neel feels a desperation rising inside him. After five minutes, the camera focuses on the mourners once more, and he sees that Annie has drifted off. The camera takes a wide shot, and in that frame, he sees her walking slowly away, like a ghost, and then stopping nearby. She bends down and picks something that on the grainy screen looks like a flower. A little ahead, she stops in front of a grave and places the flower on it. Even from this distance, he knows what she has done—she is at Hannah Arendt's resting place.

Does she know he paid tribute to Carson McCullers?
'Life, life, life ...'
He keeps saying it, till he is exhausted—of life.

*

There was so much beauty in the world. He felt moved by it, by the smallest of moments, and especially when a man put aside his conditioning and created a little magic. On his phone, he repeatedly saw a video where a child, born deaf, was able to hear for the first time with the help of an implant. Someone said, 'I am your baby sister.' And the child looked at her in astonishment and giggled. Words. Beauty. Like that Louis Armstrong song, 'What a Wonderful World', where Louis took out a handkerchief to wipe his brow and then clenched his jaw in a particular way while singing.

*

He decides to create an oasis of magic himself. The idea comes to him that perhaps he can look for a small apartment nearby. And create a home the way he wants, even if there is to be no love. Maybe things will flow from here; maybe he will be able to write again. Maybe the abdominal pain—which has reappeared—will disappear or lessen. He'll not tell anyone about the apartment. He will create a sanctuary.

He gets in touch with brokers, who show him apartments. But these are mostly old, owned by people who think of them as investments. Condemned like Sisyphus, they have been placed on rent, again and yet again, and have turned haggard. Paint peels off their walls, dogs seem to have chewed the laminate, plug points have been gouged out. They hold grimy kitchen shelves, rusty taps, leaking faucets, balconies covered with pigeon shit. One by one, he rejects them. Were he to live in one of these apartments, a new despair would rise inside him.

He tells the broker to show him newer apartments. After a few sightings, he finally likes one. Like the apartment in Yale, this one, too, is on the sixth floor. Nobody has lived there. It belongs to a young woman, who is a software engineer in America and has bought the flat with her savings. Her brother, who says he is an amateur astrologer, shows it to him. 'I had told my mother that a writer will come and live here,' he says. And then: 'This is your last birth. From here, you are free from the cycle of life and death.'

He ignores these ramblings, and quickly pays a deposit to seal the deal. The man asks for advance rent of two months; he pays this, too, without complaint.

And just like that, one morning, he is handed over the keys of an apartment where he can let go of things. He goes in, and like Adaa had done long ago, he stands in one corner of the living room, thinking about what can be done. He makes a list of things he needs. There is to be a sofa, and a couch, behind which he will put a floor lamp for adequate light to read. In the other room, he will keep a table and a chair, and a bookshelf with books he'll need immediately or old favourites—*Finding the Center*, *A Moveable Feast*, *Infinite Jest* and *Gravity's Rainbow*. There'll be plants. And light. He also needs a working kitchen—by which he means a fridge, a microwave oven and a hot plate. And coffee percolators. The one thing he absolutely requires is a kitchen smelling of coffee. It should have all kinds—especially the 80-20 (laced with chicory) variety, that transports him to his pilgrimage in the south. After putting in an honest day's work, he'll light a cigarette and listen to Samuel Barber's 'Adagio for Strings'.

He reminds himself to never forget how much beauty this world, this pale blue dot—as Carl Sagan used to call it—holds. Despite all its ugliness, greed, faux liberalism, massacres, floods, the whole inhumanness of it—there is love. It does not matter if it is not for him, as long as it pervades some aspects of the world around him.

Gradually, the place comes together. He begins referring to it as Base Camp. With a friend, he goes to Home Centre to buy curtains, and ceramic plates, and tall glasses for water, and cut glasses for whisky.

The friend, Gargi, is in a constant battle with her mother, who has, she says, always tried to pull her down. As a result, she has severe body image issues. She goes on long fasts, after which there are days where she only consumes potato wafers. Neel does not tell her, but there is a little bit of her mother in her as well. She has friends; she jokes about their ignorance of geographical facts, of politics. She is one to carry a cross, even if someone says, 'Hey, you can keep it down, you don't need to.' She will not keep the cross down but will, instead, put fluorescent markers on it, to highlight that she is carrying it.

Beneath all of this is an inner child who is beautiful. She will do just about anything for people she feels love for. She is happy to take them under her wing, like the most popular girl in a sorority.

Right this instant: she has left her busy office schedule to help Neel set up home. In many ways, she understands his thirst. Or, if she does not, she learns to accept it. In return, he embraces her madness.

So, they go and buy things.

Gargi knows about his obsession with Sage Mehta's wooden table. She takes an office colleague with her to an old furniture market and orders a similar one. It comes one day in a cargo truck, just as he is setting up the kitchen. He tears open the cover; the smell of fresh wood polish hits him. He moves two steps away to take it in. It is not what Mehta's table was, but Gargi has put in a lot of effort. And it is a good table. In honour of her gesture, he immediately begins to think of it as *his* long, wooden table.

She has also got two rugs from an artisan known to her parents. One, he puts in his study, and the effect is transformational. It is a sunny afternoon, and in the gentle breeze, the sheer curtains wave like swans. He is moved immensely. It is like that moment in his childhood, when he had hidden himself in the middle of a rose bed.

Over the years, he has collected things in the hope that someday he'll get to put them in his own house—a large orange rug, coffee mugs bought from a museum shop in Berlin, papier-mâché boxes, a silver letter opener, paper cutters (and knives) of all kinds (all!), two beautiful Van Gogh reprints, a bust of Kierkegaard, first editions of McCullers, a picture of Hemingway writing at a wooden table, a portable typewriter bought from Hyderabad, a poster of the cover of James Agee's *Let Us Now Praise Famous Men*, and a wall clock with a cow's tail as its second needle with a fly on it (a pun on 'time flies!').

The fridge arrives, and the sofa, and so does the couch. He arranges and rearranges things, flitting from one room to another, till everything makes sense to him. From the balcony, he can see other balconies, where domestic workers clean grilles and glass windows, and put clothes on the line to dry. He places a bonsai that Gargi's cat had mauled earlier. He watches the plant every day, touching it, talking to it, and giving it time to revive. Within days, it begins to sprout new leaves. He gets obsessed with cleaning—getting up, every now and then, to run the broom over a patch of dust or pick up a fallen leaf or a feather.

Gradually, like the bonsai, some essence returns to him. He continues to stay with his parents but spends his day here. Slowly, he begins to sit at the table and write. The house, as he had promised himself, smells of coffee. Everything is in order. He feels an equilibrium returning inside him, all atoms and quarks in their original place, in complete sync—like a beautiful ballet. It is not Rausch, but at least there is some peace.

In the coming weeks, a few other things arrive. Someone sends a huge indoor palm plant. Another friend gets a beautiful stone ashtray. Someone sends bed linen from Morocco. His fridge fills up with a stock of things, just like it had in New Haven with Annie. He likes to be in this apartment in solitude, surrounded by these markers of home.

Sometimes, though, the sight of the wooden table makes him sad. He can call friends over, he can have a party, but there is something incomparable about two people, two lovers, who stay back, no matter how many people come and go. It is like that passage in *A Moveable Feast*, where Hemingway tells his wife, 'And we'll never love anyone else but each other.' In a world that is so transient, some things should remain unchanged.

Some things, of course, cannot. There is ageing, and there is illness. And there is always the final change—death. Where are so many of the beautiful people he knew or knew of? Gone. No one can see them again. In dreams, sometimes, they come alive.

This is why, he thinks, it is vital to celebrate the moment, to always be in awe of its beauty ... because things will change the next instant.

And this is why it's important to find love.

Imagine a candle on the long wooden table, almost burnt to the stub. Friend are gone, drinks have been had, songs have been sung, life has been lived. And when the last car door is shut and the engine revs off, two people still have each other.

They return—they always will—no matter the part of world or the mindscape they inhabit, to that place called home.

*

Some of his people are returning to Kashmir. There is a belief that the situation has improved. Many known to him are taking their parents or even grandparents there.

But who does he take back? His is a family burdened with fear and guilt. He has given up on the idea of home, yet he feels he has not done enough to keep it alive for those he is close to.

No, this is not true; he has done everything he could have. But there is regret that Mother has suffered far too much. She has had a struggler's life. A refugee's life is tough, but even among a group of people who face similar circumstances, life is harder for some than it is for others. She took it harder. Everything became a battle for her—getting water, dealing with heat, the lack of space. Like Father, Neel fears it, too—that he won't be around when she goes.

The editor, who had sent him to the cut-off area in pursuit of the abducted collector, calls. He wants him to go to Kashmir and file a dispatch on the viability of the return of the Kashmiri Hindus. Neel has no desire to be there. His heart is not at rest. There has been no news from DK. He doesn't know what has happened to Gurupriya. He travels back to the other corner of Delhi, hoping that perhaps he'll find Jassi. But there is no sign of him. Gurnaam has gone missing, too. Neel sends an activist friend to his house. He reports that the house is locked. Neel could contact a couple of overground workers. But there has been a spate of arrests after the big encounter that made Gurupriya seek shelter at his house. There is too much vigilance.

He is asleep one morning when the doorbell rings. He wakes up with his heart pounding against his chest. He checks the wall clock; it is 4 a.m. Father comes out of his room. Neel asks him to wait. He opens the door and finds a young man outside, a helmet in his hands. He looks at Neel and hands over an envelope to him.

'What is it?' Neel warily asks.

'It's a biscuit for you,' the man replies.

Neel takes it and the man turns to leave.

Father retires. Neel goes back to his room and tears open the envelope. It's a letter from Gurupriya.

My dear, she writes, without naming him:

I am back. Sorry, there was no way of telling you earlier. There has been too much action here. M has faced a terrible loss. If possible, go and meet Satya in Hyderabad. But be very careful. There is too much repression. Some of our comrades have gone missing. The surveillance has increased to the point that we have no way of knowing about the welfare of several others. I don't know when we can see each other again. I hope you can meet M at least. But there is no way right now. I suggest that you do not even try it. But do meet Satya. We must be strong. If possible, write about us. History must remember us, even if unkindly.

He reads it again. What loss has M suffered? Gurupriya says nothing about it.

Satya is a poet, an ideologue of the rebels. He is very old now, so the police have lost interest in him.

Neel takes out a cigarette from his drawer and lights it. He will have to go to Hyderabad. But Mother is not well. A fear rises inside him, but he refuses to think about it. *He has to go to Hyderabad.*

The next morning, he lands in the city of pearls and takes a cab to Satya's house. He does not want to inform him of his arrival via telephone—it is most likely still being intercepted. His house could be under watch, too, but he has to take a chance.

As Neel enters Satya's living room, he finds a woman deep in conversation with the man; she wears a sari, and a faux leather bag lies by her side. Satya's wife sees Neel; she smiles and immediately goes to the kitchen to get him coffee. Satya is not at all surprised to see him—and this, Neel does not find surprising. Gurupriya must have used the rebel network to send Satya a message about his possible arrival.

'This is Shailaja,' Satya says, pointing to the woman with the faux leather bag. They look at each other and smile.

Shailaja and Satya converse briefly in Telugu. After coffee, Neel follows Shailaja out when she asks him to. He guesses that she is aware of who he is and why he's here. On the road outside, next to a small hospital, she flags an autorickshaw and asks the driver to take them to some locality. He does not ask anything; he knows, if she could, she'd tell him.

After about forty minutes, they enter a quiet neighbourhood. Shailaja guides the driver through a maze of lanes. At one small intersection, she asks him to stop. She insists on paying the driver. She waits till he has reversed and is out of sight. Then, they start walking.

Neel can see that she has been cautious; the address they are supposed to go to is still a few minutes away. They take a few turns, and then stop in front of a small house. An old man—he must be in his late seventies—and a woman, roughly the same age, sit in the living room. The woman is reading a newspaper; the man keeps down a book when he sees them. Their eyes light up as Shailaja approaches. It is genuine happiness that had two components, Neel later tells himself. One: the general happiness of elderly people who are glad to have some company; two: the happiness of two people invested in a zone of conflict, who think they are about to receive some good news from there.

These are M's parents, Shailaja informs Neel. She speaks to them in Telugu, after which the man says, 'You are welcome.' The old woman goes inside, and brings them tea and a homemade snack. The old man speaks. Neel hasn't asked him anything, but Shailaja must have passed on Satya's brief to him.

'I was associated with Dr Raja Rao, who was one of the founding members of the Progressive Artists' Association and a pioneer of Telugu cinema. Because of him, I got attracted to the spirit of people's theatre. After his death in September 1963, I took an oath to follow his path.

'M was born ten years later. Because my wife was an actor—we fell in love during a play that I was directing—our house used to be full of people. Writers, playwrights, actors, set designers. There would be endless discussions on art and cinema. There were books everywhere.

'M's sister was born a few years after her. M was intelligent, always a class topper. But teachers found her irritating because she'd ask too many questions and argue in the classroom. There would be complaints. When I'd tell her to stop questioning authority, she'd say, "Then why are you doing these plays where you yourself ask so many questions?" She always left me speechless.

'The younger one was quiet. She spoke less than her sister, but her head was always buried in a book. She looked up to her sister. If M wanted a pen, she'd want it too.

'One day, M came home from senior school and said she had seen a poor man foraging for food from a dustbin. She took all the snacks made by her mother and went back and gave them to him. Her mother was very angry.'

At this point, the wife says something. The man smiles.

'She says she was angry because M took away everything. There were guests coming later that day and there was nothing left for them. Upset with her mother, M refused to eat anything at all that day. The younger sister followed suit. You see, they were inseparable. My little one used to say, "Whatever Akka does, I have to do as well."

'M went to college for a bachelor's degree in political science. She was also very interested in mathematics. It was in college that she came in touch with the party. In those days, there was a young man called Pulanjaya. He was a fiery orator, who gave exhilarating speeches. M started attending his meetings. She sought admission for a master's degree, but dropped out midway. With Pulanjaya and others, she would organize mine workers in faraway districts. One of Pulanjaya's comrades had killed a rowdy man who used to harass women. The comrade had been arrested, and M and the others worked for days to put together a legal defence for him.

'By this time, it was clear to me what she was aligning herself with. I don't know exactly how, but I reconciled with it. My concerns, in any case, were different. The younger one was feeling left out and wanted to join her sister. M tried to dissuade her. She even said that one of them had to be around to live a normal life for the sake of the parents. But my younger child would not budge.

'Later that year, Pulanjaya went underground. The police kept looking for him and, to our surprise, even raided our house. But they could not find anything except books. My wife got worried. The police wanted M for questioning. One day, she came trembling back home. She was twenty-one. She said a police officer had shown her the bodies of comrades that his squad had killed. The officer had told her that soon, she would be lying on a tarpaulin sheet like this, with those who had killed her forming the backdrop.

'Strangely, after that, M became calm. She continued with her work and had several clashes with right-wing student groups. A year and a half passed this way. She'd leave early in the morning and return late. Our neighbours began to talk. But they never said anything directly to us.

'In December that year, one night, M did not return. We really got scared. I knew a police officer, and, in desperation, I called him. He was very cold. He said our parenting was flawed, and that our daughter would be in serious trouble if she did not mend her ways. My wife kept praying all night.

'M came back the next morning. Her hair was dishevelled, her eyes bloodshot. She said nothing. Her mother gave her a cup of tea. She sat right there, where you sit today. She revealed that the night before, Pulanjaya had been killed in a faraway city. The police had penetrated his inner circle, and through a mole, had poisoned his food. He and another senior leader were then picked up in an unconscious state and shot dead. This had been presented as a police encounter.

'That afternoon, M packed a small bag. She took out all the family albums and burnt pictures in which she was present. This, she declared, was to erase her identity … so that the police would find it difficult to look out for her. She met her sister in their room. We heard heated arguments. Then, M emerged. She touched our feet and asked us to forgive her. She said she had to choose this path of radicalism. She said it was up to us to convince the younger one that her life was here. That she should keep studying and apply for a master's degree. Then, she left.'

'Did you not stop M?' Neel asks.

The man goes quiet. He looks at his wife; she is staring at the floor in front of her. Shailaja holds her hand.

'My wife did not speak to me for days; she said I had failed in my responsibility,' he whispers. 'But how could I stop M? All my life, I had worked for the cause of theatre. I had never compromised on my beliefs—on what I perceived as theatre's role in people's lives. I refused to turn it into crass entertainment for the sake of money. Stopping my daughter would mean negating and nullifying all of it. Would she have respected me for that? And even if I had tried stopping her, I could see it in her eyes—she wasn't about to be reined in.

'Once I let her go, how could I stop the younger one? It would have been unfair. I couldn't possibly tell her, "Look, your sister is gone. You are the only one left. Who will take care of us? Spare a thought for us!" I couldn't have done that. She said that she had promised her Akka that she would finish her degree in English literature. The day she did, she made us sit down in this very room. She said that she had sent a message to M. Whether we liked it or not, she had the right as an individual to find her own path.

'Back then, I remember, there was so much surveillance on our house. We would go out and see men in plain clothes. We knew they were from the police, from the intelligence department. They hoped that the older one would turn up to see us. But she never did. Her letters would arrive sometimes. And then, those stopped, too.

'Finally, the younger one left. She made it a little easier for us. One day, we woke up and saw she wasn't there. She had kept a note on the table.'

A month after that, M wrote to them. She said that her sister had reached. '*Don't worry, I will take care of her*,' the missive said towards the end.

After this, the father got to meet M only on one occasion. This was several years post her departure, when a round of negotiations had taken place between the government and the rebel leaders. A message came that she was in a guesthouse in Hyderabad, where the rebel leaders had been put up. M said that only her father could come, as she would get emotional if she met her mother. She did not want that.

'I hugged her for a long time. She had reduced so much. And her hair had thinned out. I gave her a packet of sweets that I knew she liked. As I left, she said that we should consider her dead; that if it gave us peace, we could offer shraadh.'

At this moment, the mother cries, mumbling something.

'She is asking me not to say this,' the man says. 'Every day, I pick up the newspaper, dreading that I will read some bad news. Every time the phone rings, I think it must be about one of them. Or both of them.'

Neel wants to tell them about Gurupriya's dangerous journey to his house in Delhi; and that in her sleep he heard her longing for her mother. But then he thinks better of it; besides, that piece of information about Gurupriya's yearning will break the mother's heart.

'Gururpiya is fine, I met her recently,' he tells them, without divulging the details. The mother, he thinks, wants to know where, but her husband says something, after which she does not pursue it.

When it is time to leave, Neel sees that Shailaja's face has turned grim. It isn't like him, but he tells her what he has observed. She looks at him but says nothing. They continue walking outside.

'Do you mind if we walk a bit longer?' she asks.

Suddenly, she starts talking.

Some time ago, she says, something had happened. 'I don't think you are aware of it. Do you remember the death of Sudhakar?'

Of course, he replies. Sudhakar had been a senior leader of the rebels, a member of their central committee. He was the man behind several major attacks on political leaders and security forces. He had been killed six weeks earlier with another rebel leader in an encounter with the police.

'He was not killed where the police said he was,' Shailaja says. 'He was my brother-in-law. And he was M's partner.'

Neel does not know how long they walk. But they are drenched in sweat when they stop. He understands how complex matters of the heart are, and that no language, no school of psychology can codify this.

At one level, Shailaja's confession has less to do with M's life, and more to do with her own. But some things, Neel believes, cannot be picked up and seen in isolation. They are tied and remain so till the end.

Shailaja had been married to Sudhakar's elder brother. He was a college dropout and worked as a contractor, unlike Sudhakar, who studied hard and earned a gold medal in engineering. The two brothers were not close.

Sudhakar went on to choose an unusual path. He turned up at Shailaja's house a day before her wedding to his brother. He gifted her a wristwatch. It was an ordinary watch, he said, but one that would remind her that she had to build her own life and that there was to be no compromise with that. He advised her to continue her education and be independent. 'No matter how much your husband earns, you should have a little of your own,' he said. And then he disappeared under the cover of darkness. The meeting had lasted ten minutes. Shailaja got married the next day. Decked in gold, she reached her new house.

'Initially, it was all good. My in-laws were supportive. My husband was a little too fond of alcohol, but we were used to it. All around us, men were always drinking and getting aggressive. But then, I realized, in his case, it was a major problem. He could not live without liquor.'

When she confronted him, he started making excuses to stay out as much as he could. He would go on long trips, claiming that his job required that of him.

'He would return, then bring me a little gift and say he was going to change his life. But that never happened. I realized he said these things to sleep with me. He would stay for a few days, communicate by way of monologues, then hang out with his friends and come back drunk.'

One day, when he returned, Shailaja could see that he was unwell. He had lost weight and refused to look her in the eye. She thought he had started doing drugs.

'I rummaged through his bag and found a lot of prescriptions. I could not understand them. I took the prescriptions to a friend, who was a nurse, and she showed them to a doctor in her hospital. The doctor said that my husband was HIV positive.

'When I confronted him, he begged me not to tell his parents. He said that he had been visiting prostitutes and that it was most likely he had contracted the virus in a brothel. I was so naïve … it did not occur to me that he had been sleeping with me; that I could be at risk, too.

'Years of rampant alcohol abuse had already weakened his body. Eighteen months later, he was gone. In his last days, he kept asking for my forgiveness. But there was nothing to forgive. I felt as if I was crossing some dark tunnel and there was no light at the end.

'I sent a letter to Sudhakar explaining everything. I got a message back from him. A man drove me on his motorcycle to some place, and Sudhakar and I met there. Sudhakar was very supportive. He said he would put me in touch with doctors; since I was healthy, I should not worry too much. He said that I had to continue with my education and stand on my own two feet. With his support, I completed a law degree and became a lawyer.

'Sudhakar managed to keep in touch, mostly through letters. We would also meet once in six months in similar, secretive ways.

'A few weeks ago, I got a message from him. He said he couldn't come to our meeting place; that he had to be very cautious. He told me that someone would buy me a ticket and deliver it to me. I had to catch a train to a city and wait for a message at the railway station. Sure enough, a man came with a ticket. I took a small bag, put a jar of his favourite pickle in it, caught the train, and reached the city the next morning. The moment I got down, a man was waiting for me. He had me ride pillion on his bike and dropped me at a bus station. From there, he asked me to take an auto to a building. He gave me the number of the apartment; I had to remember it and not write it down anywhere. All through my journey, I kept repeating that number. Finally, I reached. The apartment was on the fifth floor. I rang the bell, and after some time, Sudhakar opened the door. He was in a shirt and trousers. The clothes were new, he said, and had been gifted to him by a friend. The whole day, we stayed in that apartment. I got up to cook, but he said I was to rest. He took care of the cooking. We had food, sitting on the floor of the room. I looked around; there was hardly anything there, except for a chair, a table and a laptop.

'In between, he exercised a bit. He said his knees were growing weak and that his uric acid levels had hit the roof. Living in jungles was taking a toll on him. He kept asking me about my life. He said that I must live well and become a good lawyer.

'That evening, we went out for a meal to a restaurant nearby. He had a masala dosa; he told me about M and how they had decided to commit to one another. He said it did not mean much in the jungle, but at least he felt loved. As he said this, I thought about how much I had longed to live a normal life with my husband, go with him to a restaurant. I did not want anything fancy—the occasional shared meal outside, a good house where I could feel at home. None of that happened.

'And here was this handsome man taking me out for a meal.

'The next morning, he left early. Before leaving, he said that if he did not return by 10 p.m., I had to vacate the flat and destroy the laptop that lay there on the table. I stayed in the house all day, imagining a life I could never have. At one point, I sensed a gentle breeze against the bedsheet that served as a curtain in the room. I felt sad.

'That night, he did not return at ten. I waited, hoping that he had somehow got delayed. I forgot that he had asked me to leave. It was midnight; he remained missing. I kept waiting for him, sitting in the kitchen, looking at the pickle jar he had left on the slab.

'At 5 a.m., I decided to open Eenadu TV's website. Right then, my world shattered. There was a news report about Sudhakar having been killed in a place far away from the city I was in. They must have picked him up and shot him there, to pass it off as an encounter.

'I quickly picked up the laptop and ran away. I got to a bridge over the Godavari and threw the laptop into the river.'

She stops here.

'You know, I have never met M. But if Sudhakar's absence were to be counted in atoms, my heart will have them more than hers,' she says.

Neel places his hand on her shoulder. She closes her eyes for a second.

'Oh, I forgot,' she says, putting her hand into her bag. 'I got this for you.'

It is a packet of sweets with the bespectacled man on it. Even in the midst of so much grief, she has made a gesture for a man who shares a connection with those people she values.

In a way, through that bespectacled man, they have all become one.

*

Neel is back at home. Mother's eyes shine, as they always do, when she sees him. She manages to convey that her back hurts. He rubs it.

The next day, she has an unusual look on her face; it is without expression. He talks to her, cracks a few jokes, tells her that she has to eat more; that the next morning, he will take her out to the balcony. These things usually make her smile, but that day she just looks at him, as if he's speaking an alien language.

Around 10.15 that night, she crosses over while he is holding her. They had been expecting it. But when it happens, the pain in Neel's heart reminds him nothing could have prepared him for it. He cannot bear to look at Father's face who is in the room and sits by himself. Even when Neel is not looking at him, he can see a million lines of grief being carved on his face.

There is a photo of his parents in one of the Mughal gardens in Kashmir Valley taken right after their marriage. In it, they stand next to each other; she is taking the support of Father's sturdy shoulder and holds his hand tightly. Tonight, she has to travel far by herself.

Someday, they will all be together again.

After the rituals are done and the relatives are gone, he goes to *Love's Work*, to the poem that the author Gillian

Rose's friend sent her. It is by Pier Paolo Pasolini, and is called 'Prayer to My Mother'. There is a stanza that goes:

Only you in all the world know what my
heart always held, before any other love.

So, I must tell you something terrible to know:
From within your kindness my anguish grew. [...]

And I don't want to be alone. I have an infinite
hunger for love, love of bodies without souls.

He begins to cry.

*

That night, he wakes up with a deep, bottomless longing for Mother. He has a strong desire to hold her, to tell her why she has been in bed for so long.

Get up, Mother, won't you make me lemonade?

Then it dawns on him that she is gone; that she has passed like mist passes. She leaves nothing behind, except her saris and a watch with a big white dial that does not have a single scratch.

*

He vacates Base Camp. All the beautiful things go into cartons. Fifteen days later, he is with Father for a check-up in a hospital. He feels the walls closing in on him. It is a panic attack, but he cannot tell Father. He paces up and down the corridor, as patients and attendants swarm around him.

After some time, the feeling goes away.

*

He is in Chandigarh at Gurnaam's invitation. This is a public event, and he has been asked to speak. Some of Gurnaam's friends associated with the labour movement have organized it. He reaches a day earlier and finds that his stay has been arranged as in the old days, in a community building. The manager is a labour rights activist and he has managed to set aside a bed for Neel on one side of a large hall, where there are pictures all around of comrades who fell to the bullets of Sikh extremists. Neel is old now; he is unable to live like this. He picks up his bag quietly and takes a room in a hotel nearby.

The next morning, he goes to the venue and speaks about the struggles of the Adivasis in central and eastern India. Afterwards, a comrade, a friend of Gurnaam's, tries to hand an envelope to him, which has some cash in it.

'I cannot take this,' Neel says, and pushes it towards him. 'I came here at Gurnaam's invitation. I do not take money from him or his friends.'

He can see Gurnaam's eyes lighting up with pride. The gesture means a lot to him; Neel knows it.

After the event, Gurnaam takes Neel to a room in the building. Tea arrives.

'How are you, Neel?' he asks.

'I am okay.'

'No, I mean, really, how are you?'

What can he tell him? Even if he were to try, he wouldn't find the right idiom for heartbreak. The pain that overwhelms him each time he remembers Mother is easier to share.

'I cannot get over my grief, Comrade.'

Gurnaam nods; he understands. He takes out a pack of cigarettes and offers one to Neel. Neel takes it, and they both sit in silence, smoking and taking sips of tea.

'I lost my mother when I was eight; I still dream of her,' Gurnaam says. 'Give it time; it will become better. But it won't leave you completely.'

Neel changes the subject. 'Where is Jassi?'

'Jassi is in DK now,' Gurnaam says. 'Things are not good there. The state forces are going deeper and deeper for operations. I am waiting to get my niece married … then I will go.'

Gurnaam's sister had assigned her daughter's responsibility to him before she died. Neel is aware of this. A few moments later, he gets up.

'Are you leaving?' Gurnaam asks.

'Yes, Comrade, I have to go. I don't know how Mother's death has affected Father. He does not talk much. I need to be with him.'

'Take care of your father … and don't worry,' Gurnaam smiles.

They hug.

From behind his thick glasses, his eyes shine.

'Here, this is for you,' Gurnaam says as he hands over an envelope to him.

Neel opens it and finds a flower pressed in it.

I am thinking of you. I am very sorry about the loss of your Amma. I remember the spark in her eyes whenever I'd mention you. I had this urge sometimes to make her sit on a chair and apply oil to her hair. But I feared that it would make me weak. On my last day, you made me weak with the mention of home, with the dream of settling down. But it's late; it's too late to dream about such things. Take care of yourself. And come and see me when you can. Love, G.

*

Sometime in the beginning of the following year, Aarani sends Neel a link to a *New York Times* report of two Auschwitz prisoners—also lovers—who reunited seventy-two years after being separated. Around the same time, the web series based on his book is also aired.

In February that year, Neel gets a message from Aarani. 'Sometimes I feel like I still own you.' It brings to the fore a particular memory that has eluded him all these months. At one point, in the hotel room they had shared in Mumbai, in response to something he had said, Aarani had laughed, 'You are my doormat.' It had sent him into a tizzy. He felt as though she had made him drink a potion, after which all he could remember was her name. She had said it in a playful manner, but it touched him deeply, as if it were the offering of a sacrament.

He writes back to her: 'I continue to be your doormat.'

'To what end?'

'That I have no clue about. I am saying what I feel. Just like you are.'

'You should do that more often.'

There is no communication between them till June. By this time, the pandemic is raging and people are struggling to make sense of the world around them. Like most others, he is working from home, doing his share of Zoom calls, trying his best to keep afloat.

In June, Aarani sends him a picture of a tablet strip. Via a Google search, he finds out that it is a mood stabilizer.

The picture is followed by a message: 'With you, I felt safe for the first time in my life, and then I didn't.'

'And then you didn't. Why?' Neel replies.

'Because you abandoned me. I should have known that I've always been unlovable.'

'Come on, Aarani. You are not unlovable. I loved you with all my heart. Something got stuck between us that night and we couldn't come out of it.

He wants to be in Mumbai that very instant, throw away her medication and tell her that he will heal her. He will take away all her pain.

That night, she sends him another message. It is late; he knows she has been drinking far too much.

'You have nothing more to say?'

I have a lot to say, Aarani. But I am unable to.

*

As the first wave of Covid ebbs, he decides to change home. It will be his first decent house—a house where he could have offered Mother a life she would have cherished. For Father, it won't make much of a difference; he has a concept of home, but it does not necessarily have to be a *good house*, the way Neel sees it. His idea of a home is having everyone he loves around him.

Gargi comes visiting with a box of Baklava once he shifts. 'This is your final act,' she says. By this, she means that he can live here for the rest of his life; this is as good as it gets. The apartment is in a new part of the city, in a gated community, where residents are obsessed with finding efficient house help and where children have strange names—the internet claims these have been derived from the Vedas, but they haven't really. People have big cars but, for the most part, small hearts. There is a community messaging group, where if one person happens to write, 'A man fell from the thirtieth floor,' the next message will read, 'Moving out sale!'

But there is a manicured lawn, and twenty-four-hour security, and uninterrupted power supply. There is a little Venetian bridge over a grassy mound, a part of the landscaping, beneath which teenage boys and girls steal kisses. In the morning, groups of old men and women take walks, and participate in activities like laughter yoga, and exchange notes on how to reduce hypertension. Father has no interest in these gatherings. He goes down once every morning to walk alone, and then returns as fast as he can. From across the gypsum-filled wall, Neel hears the weak trickle of his piss; he thinks: I will get there eventually.

Gargi is aware of Neel's history. She has been with him in chock-full auditoriums, where he has read passages from his book on the exile, sometimes banging the table to force people to *see* his anger.

There are things she'll understand if he tells her. He can tell her that he often dreams of the house he has been severed from, and its red-oxide corridor; that he imagines he's levitating, hovering over it, as if he were wearing a jetpack. He can tell her that it was in this house that he learnt how to ride a bicycle; that, one night, he dreamt of riding it, before he actually knew how.

But he has no language at his command to convey these thoughts. He cannot find a proper idiom to tell her that even in his childhood house something felt amiss; something ached like a phantom limb. The house had many rooms; yet, his struggle was to create a space where he could feel at home. He tried to create an illusion of it sometimes, by placing bedsheets over chairs and tables, and decorating them with flowers and whatever else he could find.

Still: home remained distant.

*

In the new apartment, he walks to the closet in the bedroom, and imagines Aarani's things there.

What happened between them?

'You need to heal,' Aarani had told him one day, when they were still together. 'You go silent in between, you know,' she explained.

They had been talking, and for a few minutes, there had been a pause. He was comfortable with it. Clearly, she found the silence jarring.

'So, what do you want to talk about?' he had asked.

There was no response.

Aarani never talked about her time in London, her childhood, her school. He'd see her flipping through the pages of the *Economist*, but she would never speak of her impression of the things she read. He had no idea, for example, what she thought of the events in the Middle East, or of the burgeoning immigration crisis, or of the new, fascinating findings on migration into India. She did not even talk about her own work, beyond office politics.

And her diagnosis was: he needed to heal.

Silence came naturally to Neel. It was something vital—a pause; a transition from one thought to another; a mind-cleanser, a remover of the debris of useless words; a caesura between an old conversation and a new one.

Aarani saw it as something malefic. The silence, which was meant to be light, became an encumbrance.

*

One morning, in June, all of it ends. It ends in about five seconds.

He opens Instagram and finds Aarani in her trousseau, a tiara of gold around her head. She looks like a Chola princess. Her hair is wound tightly—the same hair she would ask him to comb with his fingers in Mumbai cabs, especially while they crossed the Sea Link.

He cannot look at anything, except this picture. A strange weakness overtakes his body. He crumbles, withers and degrades. The elephant of Alexander's army comes down with a thousand burning arrows.

He feels dizzy; his tongue dries up.

It is heartbreak. It is what shatters gods and brings empires down. It can cause locust showers, make maggots appear in magnificent pears, stun fish in the Atlantic, cause nosebleeds, turn hair grey in seconds, suck out the yellow from a Van Gogh painting. Fifty-eight push-ups turn to five.

He is dying. He has nothing, he is nothing. He should roll in dust, he should beat his chest. He should invoke Batalvi's hawk and ask it to gouge his eyes out. He should throw himself to the crocodiles.

*

It hits him in his gut—the spectacle of her being lifted on shoulders, garlanding the groom, wearing what he always imagined she would on their wedding day.

But it is someone else she's marrying. Someone named Brian.

She has the same sweet smile on her face, her cheeks like tomatoes, as if she hasn't forsaken her aerobics class even on her wedding day.

He feels like a gazelle wounded by a gunshot. He cannot cry, he cannot speak, he cannot breathe; his body is a beaten-up chunk of meat.

He hits upon an idea. He will message her. He sends her three messages on WhatsApp in quick succession.

I cannot overcome my grief. I feel like rolling on the floor. I feel like tattooing your name all over my body like the Ramnamis.

He quickly thinks of ways of making her come back to him.

Okay, I will talk non-stop. There won't be a moment of silence. I will be like that jukebox at Café Mondegar. Come back; save me from the tempest of your parting.

Suddenly, he wonders: what's the moment when my stoicism turned into a slut and abandoned me?

He can't be stoic.

I imagine that outside your neighbourhood there will be a map and a tiny little dot that says: you are here. I want to be there. How do I get you back?

In panic—he likes to believe it is panic and not disgust—she blocks him on WhatsApp.

He could not possibly have harmed her in any way; he would kill himself before doing that. There are torrents of words that come to him, and he wants to relay them to her.

I have checked your Instagram stories a million times. I have a dead animal stuck in my throat. I feel an immense sense of loss, bereavement.

Should I petition Change.org to get you back?

In desperation, he puts a rubber band—in which his *Indian Express* comes wrapped—on his wrist. Every time he remembers Aarani or has an urge to go to her Instagram page, he snaps it.

Still, he ends up thinking of her. His heart hurts; his wrist turns into a blue mess.

He goes out for a run, hoping it will revive him. His Garmin watch displays a performance condition of minus five. His Vo2 Max goes down by a point.

If she comes back, I will marry her immediately. In a temple, mosque, church, synagogue, Times Square, Machu Picchu. I will do one thousand circumambulations of Shirdi. Why am I not friends with Shah Rukh Khan? I would have asked him to invite her and tell her that there is a man who loves her and is dying with grief.

What has happened to him? He closes his eyes. He sees her, a bride. Her photo in the bridal outfit has strayed too close to his world, to his aesthetic universe. It is the same aesthetic that had overwhelmed him the day they met at the Chennai airport—of them together in the kovil.

As he opens his eyes, the vision takes a sharp swerve and goes to Brian.

Brian … of all people, she had to marry a man called Brian? Brian, the fucking goat!

He is unable to eat. He cannot smoke a cigarette or have a drink—he suddenly develops a deep distaste for such diversions. It is as if Aarani's private Christ wants him to suffer.

Snap.

There is a picture of her. A friend, whom he now stalks on Instagram, has put it up. Her legs, the same legs he had held in his for nights. The diamond ring glitters in the semi-darkness of the hotel bar.

Snap, snap.

He checks the picture again. God! Her right hand is on Brian's thigh.

Snap, snap, snap.

He messages Tanya, the producer of his OTT show. In the illusory and fake world of Bombay cinema, she is the only one he can be friends with. He looks at Aarani's bridal photos once more. Then he calls Tanya in alarm, not knowing what else to do.

'Is there a Sai temple in Mumbai?'

'I am sure there is. Go to Siddhivinayak. Offer the god a coconut.'

'I will offer him my head as a coconut if she comes back.'

'Message her. Ask her to meet. Get her something.' Then: 'Have you eaten?'

'I have got ulcers in my mouth, Tanya. I am surviving on buttermilk.'

'No one likes to kiss a mouth with ulcers.'

'I have no one.'

'Thanks to you, I stalked her on Instagram.'

'She is a baby.'

'Ha ha.'

'Small baby.'

'Accha, eat something now. And demand that she meets you—not for five minutes, but for an hour.'

*

Should he just disappear, and emerge after five years as someone who has learnt hatha yoga, with all desire gone? He could be like Tirumalai Krishnamacharya in that old black-and-white video. He could appear, one fine day, on a small patch of grass on some hillock, performing asanas, looking calm, taking out his tongue like a lion ...

But what if she calls?

No, he cannot disappear.

*

He forgets he is forty-six. In a few years, he will be fifty. No pace, no running cadence of 190 SPM, no squats, no deadlifts, will change that fact.

Will Aarani move to London with Brian?

Snap, snap, snap.

*

He thinks of what this entire period has felt like. It has felt like a cloudburst. Or like being hit by a meteor.

When she felt love, she used to call him 'Mister'.

'How many words today, Mister?'

'Say you love me, Mister.'

*

She responds angrily on Instagram. He immediately relays it to Tanya.

'There is a spring back in your voice,' Tanya says.

Ah, yes. Aarani has responded. A response means she feels something ... even if that something is anger.

'I am a married woman now,' she writes.

It makes him laugh—this sudden Victorian sensibility.

'No, I will not meet you. Do not message me.'

No reply or blocking means death. She is responding, and that means hope.

*

For a day, she posts nothing. He keeps checking, hoping to catch a glimpse.

Tanya is optimistic. 'She must be happy inside,' she says.

'Happy?'

'Yes. Who does not want to know that they are loved like this? And she must also be delighted to see you suffer.'

This makes him happy. She may turn back and retrace her steps. He loves her and she will come to realize that her life is with him.

He reaches the airport early. The flight is at 2 p.m., but he is there at 11.15. The rubber band stays; no metal detector cares about it. After security check, there is still over an hour to kill. He doesn't know how he will face Mumbai. It's the city he's travelling to. He walks into the bar and orders a double gin and tonic. The image of Aarani as a bride flashes before him; he snaps his rubber band. The lone bartender sees him do it. He is young, inclined to talk sweetly to his customers, who are mostly there for a snack before their flights. A man hovers near him, looking at the bar menu. The cost of drinks dissuades him. Neel almost offers to pay, but the man quickly walks away before he can engage. Neel orders another.

'How many words did you write today, Mister?'

'None, Aaru. I am finished.'

Snap.

'Say you love me, Mister.'

'Oh, I love you, Aaru. I love you.'

*

The OTT platform that has released his web series has invited him for an event—they are celebrating something; something that he cannot remember. He wears a white shirt and jeans; he sits in Tanya's big car and they reach the venue, a hotel near the airport. On a counter inside, he is asked his name, which the door supervisors then check against a guest list. They tie a paper band around his wrist, as if he's seeking entry into a nightclub. There are a million people inside. He moves through the crowds; every now and then, he spots a familiar face. One of them, a good actor, stands alone. In the melee, no one seems to care about him. A young star, who has recently featured in a web series, is clicking pictures with girls. One of them is in a beige leather skirt—it reminds him of Shailaja's bag the day he met her in Hyderabad.

There is a huge crowd at the bar. Cutting through this takes time, and when he finally reaches the counter, he asks for a whisky. An old actor he knows, and who is looking for somebody to stand with, spots him and squeezes next to him. The actor begins to talk. Neel cannot hear a word. But he nods. On the screen, they show his photo among writers and actors. Then a band begins to play; the lead singer starts with Kabir's dohas. No one is paying heed. In five minutes, Neel is out, walking towards the smoking area—he badly needs a cigarette. Tonight, Tanya cannot be with him—she has to mingle with the biggies in the party.

He returns to the hotel room, without having eaten a morsel. He opens a miniature from the minibar and a packet of cashews. It is 1.30 a.m. In the adjacent room, through the thin wall, he can hear a bunch of youngsters. They are most likely drinking and arguing. He does not understand the drift of the argument, but he hears one of them clearly.

'I am done with love,' the man says. 'I need physical love. Physical, physical, physical.'

*

Aarani wants it like dopamine, Tanya says. She wants to know how much you are suffering. She has messaged you for this reason precisely. She wants closure … but don't give her too much indication of how you are suffering. Or it will lose its meaning.

I want to give it to her as much as she desires, he says.

'Is this because she is unattainable right now? What if she happens to be available tomorrow?' Tanya asks.

He looks at her like she is a lunatic.

'There are two ways of looking at it,' Tanya continues, taking a measured sip of her margarita. 'One is to imagine that she's available, and then think about whether you'd still want to be with her. The other is to first *make* her available, and then think about whether you'd want to be with her. Personally, I prefer the second option.'

It is the evening after the OTT platform celebration. Tanya takes him from one Mumbai bar to another. He stumbles back into his hotel room around midnight.

He wakes up less than four hours later with a crick in his neck and a severe hangover. He changes into his running clothes. His whole body revolts, but he wants desperately to overcome this feeling of ill-ease. He looks out of the window, the sky is overcast, and it is drizzling. Past the American Consulate, more clouds are coming his way. Less than a hundred metres away, there is a bookshop that has wanted him for an event. But, today, he does not know how he will face an audience. He steps out, past the reception, and past the gate where they enact the mindless exercise of opening car trunks. He follows the synthetic red and green track and begins a slow run.

He takes a right turn, and finds a crew of people in fluorescent yellow vests, cleaning up puddles of water, emptying them out. A little ahead, a few barriers; after which, he spots people in identical blue jerseys, with bib numbers attached to their chests. A marathon is about to start. He picks up speed. At the next turn, some policemen are surprised to see him; they confuse him for a participant in a marathon that is yet to begin. He picks up more speed. By the time he finishes one loop, he spots two elite runners who have taken the lead, followed by a scooter escort. The runners look grim, their arms swing together, their jaws remain clenched. After he has run a few more miles, he sees a young volunteer, who waves towards a turn.

U-turn, sir, she shouts.

I cannot, my friend. I have to run straight, he feels like telling her.

But he takes the turn. He is running faster now. Unlike marathons in Delhi, this is a sombre one. There are no DJs, no national flags, and no songs mimicking the ones they play along the Indo-Pak border in Amritsar. The roads are awash, and a beam of light begins to appear in the sky. Seven. Ten. Thirteen kilometres. Two hours later, he stops. He has done twenty-two kilometres. He walks on the road. By the side, young labourers appear with their vests and safety helmets, on their way to work at construction sites. His neck is sore; he imagines Aarani touching it and rubbing it. He closes his eyes and keeps walking. She is less than five miles away. If he breaks into a sprint, he will be at her place in forty-five minutes. He wants to see her face, tomato red. Like some abandoned child, who can only remember the name of his street, he keeps repeating Jaun Elia's '*Be-naam Fariha*' in his head.

He recalls the mandarin in Barthes's *A Lover's Discourse*, who falls in love with a courtesan. She tells him that if he spends a hundred nights waiting for her, she shall be his. On the ninety-ninth night, though, something breaks inside him, and he walks away.

For Aarani, he would wait a thousand nights.

*

He walks aimlessly along Mumbai's streets, through Kala Ghoda, crossing Colaba, past Harbour View, and the Gateway of India, and the sea of people clicking photos. He has changed hotels and is now in this part of Mumbai.

He ends up drinking again. He cannot sleep. The next morning, he is out at Marine Drive. It is raining. The early morning walkers and laughter clubs are gone. The sealine is taken up by young couples. The men all look alike—there is glee in their eyes. There are a few loners as well. They sit with their spines erect, gazing at a boat in the distance or at tall buildings. A straight back, he thinks, means that they have decided to let go and are now trying to fix their lives through meditation and yoga and by quitting alcohol and cigarettes.

Here he is, having lost everything, but unable to let go. He is powerless, the antithesis of Bhiku Mhatre.

He runs, the smell of fish rising out of the sea to his left. He crosses a woman in rags, deep in conversation with a dog and with dozens of pigeons that come and go as they please. He runs past an old man, who has a portable karaoke—a passer-by has stopped by his side to sing a Rafi song.

That night, after leaving Café Mondegar, Aarani and he had watched a procession of Krishna devotees dancing on the street outside. Later, a eunuch had approached them, calling Aarani 'Kareena'. He had laughed and given her a hundred-rupee note.

Now, he remembers the small beads of sweat on Aarani's face and her always imperfect lipstick.

*

One evening, during his first visit to Mumbai to meet her, they are walking in Bandra when the strap of her sandal breaks. They go to a store nearby, where she points to a pair she wants, the kind that's sensible in Mumbai rains. He buys it for her, and she smiles so much, and they are both tickled by the thought (he assumes it is a shared thought) that their future selves are buying sandals. Husband. Hubby. Baby. Papi.

Later, she walks into a departmental store to buy chewing gum. He looks at her from outside. Her phone is in the back pocket of her jeans; she stands on her toes, as she takes the packet from the shopkeeper. He feels a tide of love wash over him; he is overcome by the desire to have a pet name for her. Aarani. Aaru. Baby. Aaru. Aaru. Aaru.

Niko Kolodny speaks of such moments; of an 'intensity of engagement'. These happen at unexpected times, like when a beloved laughs or gestures in a certain way.

Afterwards, Aarani and he walk over to Toto's. It is such a small and cramped place, but he is happy. The barman, who has served him in the past, recognizes him.

'Sir, where did you go? Long time,' he smiles.

Neel recalls his name. 'Nice seeing you around, Rohit.'

When the barman leaves, Aarani looks at Neel. 'You remember everything,' she says.

I remember everything. The first time I had a soft drink and the gas escaped my nose. I remember the teacher I fell in love with, and for years preserved a cotton-ball she had removed nail paint with. I remember how I came home drunk one night and howled over Rituparno Ghosh's 'Piya Tora Kaisa Abhimaan'. I remember snowfall on a March evening—I was nine years old—an experience so personal that I still can't write about it. I remember a young boy in Baghdad pointing his pistol at me; I covered my head—a silly reflex—and when nothing happened for a few seconds, I looked up, and he was gone.

These memories will surface later. Right now, he is happy, just happy, to be with Aarani.

Sometimes, he feels envious of his own self. From across the bar, a couple stares at him and Aarani. There is a man in the vicinity; he is accompanied by two women. Their touch is impersonal; they are colleagues, most likely. The man tells them that he cannot marry the woman he loves because she is Muslim.

Neel steps out with Aarani; it is midnight. Her hand is in his. He can overcome all chaos. He has an armour no bullet can penetrate.

They walk towards the spot where the last of the taxi drivers are waiting for late-night passengers. They get into a cab; the driver gets a call. It is most likely his child. He says something to the child in Marathi. Aarani drops Neel off at the hotel. They kiss and embrace.

'What do we have?' she asks.

'We have magic,' he says.

*

He spends days in Delhi conspiring: how can he get her back?

He knows her; she will be unhappy with Brian. He can see it in her eyes. He imagines that she will long for Mumbai too. He has to make her aware of what she is missing. But how? He has to build her a cathedral of peacock feathers and put his beating heart inside it. He has to light a candle outside for her, so she won't pass it by. And once she knows what she means to him, he has to be Mr Dependable.

Days pass. Her posts stop appearing, which also means he cannot see her.

One day, a panic rises within him. She is gone—and gone to a place that is not here. He cannot get up, and run to the airport, and frequent all the places she loves, till he finds her.

She will never touch him. He will not be able to hear her voice, tinged with the accent of her native place, across the table.

Suddenly, he thinks of time, of the mathematical equations that try spanning all of eternity. He thinks of the beauty of John Nash.

Should he drop everything and return to mathematics?

Or should he just get up and begin a long, excruciating run to London?

She'll wake up one day, and, over a breakfast of toast and marmalade, see a photo in the *Guardian*: 'Man Walks from Delhi to London for Love'.

Will she remember Shakespeare's 'Sonnet 116'?

Will she dwell on Patrick Hamilton's *Hangover Square* or Naipaul's *The Enigma of Arrival*?

Darkness, darkness.

In the days to come, she acts in ways that he considers strange. She blocks him on Instagram. Then, unblocks him.

Tanya is right—she wants him to see her new life and eat his heart out.

The day she unblocks him, he goes to her stories. There she is, with Brian, her arm tight around his waist. She looks a little ashen ... or is that just his imagination?

What will she do in London?

Surely, he is on her mind. 'I am in her head, I am in her head,' he repeats to himself.

The memory of his hand on her breast stays.

Maybe he will shift to London. Maybe he'll become a barman in a hotel and write at night. How will she respond if she sees him there—in a bar, with Brian and his friends? She'll spot him and her face will fall. Then she'll compose herself and participate with some enthusiasm in a conversation; with humour that is not humour at all. Perhaps he will send her a message from his phone.

Hey, you know this joke you cracked? It sucks. But you know what, I love you. Just come to this side, baby. We will take an Air India flight back to Mumbai, and I will never be honest about your jokes again. In fact, I will bend over with laughter. I will make you food your DNA is used to. I will take you to Toto's.

Despair again.

He must come to his senses. She is gone. She is married. She wants him to suffer for a short period, and then it won't matter to her. Her children will be blond. They will call her Mama. She will put pictures of them celebrating Diwali in Fabindia outfits, and Brian will wear a kurta.

Sometimes, he thinks that all this is a dream, and that he will wake up and nothing will have changed.

He will write all the beautiful mathematical equations that exist on a white board and explain them to her.

A month later, he is again at the airport, on his way back to Mumbai. There is no Aarani. There is no possibility, not even a dim one, that he will enter a pub and find her there. Maybe he will find a friend of hers, and implore the friend to talk to Aarani; tell her that her life is here, not there. That no one makes South Indian filter coffee, the 80-20 variety, like he does; that she cannot survive without it, in a cold place where people call each other 'Hoy'.

He goes to the bar in the airport, where the young bartender is at work. The bartender recognizes him.

'Sir, G and T, no?'

Neel sits with the drink; around him are passengers eating food.

He imagines that, like Pynchon's Prairie, he has access to Takeshi's visiting card. He imagines Takeshi managing it for him, tracking Aarani down in a London tube. He imagines him mumbling an ancient chant in her ear, which brings her back.

He imagines, then, taking her to Nara; she's wearing a kimono. He imagines a deer coming close to them, as they hold hands and watch the cherry blossoms.

He imagines taking her to Chidambaram, to the goddess at the Thillai Nataraja Temple. He imagines a lamp being lit before sunrise, and Aarani coming alive against its light with her measured smile (but never measured for him when they are alone). He imagines them living nearby, going to the kovil every day, listening to the young boys chanting, 'Namakam Chamakam'.

While waiting for the boarding call, he takes out his little notebook and writes:

> *I wish there were an invisible trellis in the middle of the city. When the first lockdown took place, and after the diesel fumes and the dust from construction sites had settled, I woke up and missed the gossamer of your voice so much that an alligator appeared in my coffee mug. The sound of the stone-cutting machine is back, and it never leaves me. My friends joke that in my past birth, I must have murdered a mason. Even if I go to the forest, someone will find a ruse to construct*

something there and the machine will follow. But, back then, when everything went quiet, the air had suddenly become so clean that you could see the Himalayas from Delhi's terraces. Now, of course, there is nothing to see except murderous mobs on X, raring to drown you in patriotic effluvium. You say: 'I am sick of this country'; they say: 'Bastard, go to Pakistan!' I don't want to go to Pakistan. I don't want to be home, either, where everything is dishevelled like Jaun Elia's hair. Every day something is breaking, like Elia said it did in his house, and the detritus is making my knees bleed. I want to climb that trellis. And I want to climb so high that I can see you touching the waters of the Thames. And then, I want to appear in your coffee mug, if I have to. Maybe I want to say, 'I am sick of this country,' and have someone shout back, 'Bastard, go to London!' So, I get onto that trellis, and grow wings, and fly over the Hindu Kush, and drop bombs over all the stone-cutting machines, instead of children, and come to you and say, 'Hoy.'

He boards the plane. The pilot says something indecipherable. Air hostesses walk up and down the aisle. A bald man, who is working on some Excel sheet, hands his cold towel back to a young air hostess. 'It is not cold … do you people even check it?' She takes it back. He thinks about the man. This is his way of telling himself that he has arrived. Later, he keeps making things difficult. He asks for water, for extra ice in his Coke, for a stirrer—always rudely. After a while, the air hostesses stand together near the service area. One of them looks at the man, mumbles something, and they all laugh.

The flight lands; to Neel's right are the blue tin roofs of slums. Outside: chaos. He stands in queue for a cab and finally gets one. 'Bandra,' he says. He remembers the last time he had met Aarani here, about a year after the fissure.

He had come for an Asia Society event to talk about DK. After the event, he messaged Aarani. She sent him the coordinates of a hotel. In thirty minutes, he was at Rang Sharda. He found her in the vast terrace, sitting alone, her whole body tense. A lone waiter stood in a corner and was almost surprised to see him. To Neel, it looked as though the waiter were attending to some mendicant in a forest, who was not to be disturbed, and he had entered like a wild boar.

They hugged, and he sat on a chair. He was now facing Lilavati Hospital. In the dim lights of what looked like a hospital corridor, there was the silhouette of a man, walking slowly, precisely, ten steps towards his right, then back.

'How are you?' she asked.

'I wish I knew.'

'Well ...' she replied and left it there.

There was a moment of silence, after which he immediately switched the subject of conversation to the comic relief provided by some Mumbai-based stand-up comedians. It was a topic that she could dwell on for some time. The waiter brought him a beer.

He wanted to hold her, to take the pain out of her body, from her lips—he imagined the lips turning violet. He wanted to lift her magenta shirt and run his finger over the parallelogram-shaped birthmark above her navel.

He did nothing.

*

Tanya takes him to a bar. He does not know what to do. He wants to take Aarani's hand in his. There is a beautiful line by Kedarnath Singh about holding the beloved's hand: '*Uska haath apne haath mein lete hue maine socha, duniya ko haath ki tarah garam aur sundar hona chahiye.*' He thinks of relaying it to Tanya—as I took her hand in mine, I felt that the world ought to be warm and beautiful like it—but Tanya barely understands Hindi. She understands, however, the pain and agony of a heart in love.

'I don't want to drink,' he tells Tanya.

'Don't be a lily arse,' she says.

This makes him laugh; it cuts through his despair.

He orders an Old Fashioned. Afterwards, he is glad that he has. He watches Tanya take a call. She is speaking in beautiful Marathi to a friend's mother, who is concerned about her daughter who underwent surgery recently. From what he gathers, she tells the mother not to worry; she is taking care of her friend.

There is a clarity that Tanya has about many things. She is seeing someone, but is certain that all love affairs are temporary. She must be a few years younger than Neel; yet, she has booked herself a suite in an upcoming old-age home on the outskirts of Mumbai. She is practical about it. She is the one he will approach if he wants to die; he knows she is capable of putting him on a drip of morphine.

They end up drinking till 1.30 a.m., after which they are thrown out of the pub.

He had been wary of Aarani's drinking. But he has not given it a break himself.

*

It is November, and despite the poison in Delhi's air, he is thankful to be in the city. He has stopped drinking. He keeps plants on the south-facing windowsill, makes his coffee and reads.

He will have to live.

In between, he checks on Aarani. But for weeks, there has been nothing. It could only mean two things—she is regretting her decision; or she is busy making a new life with her husband. He imagines them together in a tiny apartment, with a washing machine and a dryer, and with a TV that plays sports, while they drink beer.

As though his imagination is shaping reality—a photo appears. Of Aarani and Brian watching *Julie & Julia*. The room she is in is dark, but against the light of the TV, he can see a bottle of wine on the table.

This picture grows in his head. He can feel on his face the heat of Julia Child's stove. He puts the phone away. It feels like a finality, like the death of the African violets in his Yale apartment.

*

Time wears on. The contours of Annie's face begin to blur. The apartment in New Haven feels like a dream. He tries remembering the cold outside; and inside, the warmth of Annie's body, the assurance of her thigh pressed against his as they watch a film on David Foster Wallace. He tries to remember images through sound—the clanging of change in the homeless person's bowl; the guttural cries of Black men getting shoved into police cars; the church organs in the evening; Annie's voice whispering, 'We are one now, we are one.'

*

The epidemic of talking. People just talk, talk, talk. And they do not listen.

He wanders through this mass of humanity, from one person to another, as if bound by some inexplicable treaty to hear them out, to let them inject the dross of their lives into his veins. They speak of abusive fathers or glorious fathers, of abusive husbands or husbands they cannot figure out, of friends. Of who said what to whom.

The same old jokes repeated ad nauseam, without any awareness of their repetitive nature.

He wants to reject such talk; he wanders away.

*

Spring passes; a new summer arrives.

He drowns in mundane things. The air conditioners need servicing; the microwave oven plate is wobbly. Father repeatedly tells him that his debit card has expired. All this means multiple conversations with call centres, telling things over and over again.

There are also vague signs that Aarani is happy; or at least she is trying. There's a blurred picture of her with a dog. In another photo, she is pretending to fly on a broom like a wizard, next to a signboard that reads: 'Welcome to Broom Hill.' In yet another, with a Mumbai friend of hers, she's drinking at the pier. There's one with her face towards the sea, wearing a crimson puffer gilet; and a photo, in some busy street in London, where she's holding a red-coloured toy bus with 'Tower Bridge London' written on it.

It is unfair on his part. He should be happy for her.

He feels old; he thinks of moments when people did give up. Walter Benjamin gave up in Portbou.

He should have gone to her, taken her hand in his, and said, 'Look, I love you. Nothing should come between us. No shadows of the past, no demons from the future. Everything will be good and shiny. It will be safe. I have no sorrow nerve; I have no sorrow. I can absorb all pain; I am a black hole. I will never grow old; I promise you will die before me.'

*

Where will he find her?

He tries imagining that from now, till the moment he dies, he will never see her again.

He runs to the forest behind his house. A deep despair has been stirred inside him. It brings him to his knees in the middle of the forest. Everything collapses, all indices of control crash. He howls his heart out. There is no one here. The only other sound is that of a plane flying overhead, and then, of a cowbell, somewhere not too far.

He cries: *Oh Aarani, oh Aarani, I have fucking lost you. Why do I get this paralysis? I will surgically remove my sorrow nerve, just come back. I will take all your medicines along with you—all your mood stabilizers. We will buy a pill dispenser, come back. It is raining in Bandra. I will buy you sandals, come back. We will go to Toto's and drink till they throw us out, come back. You hate red roses. I will eradicate them from this planet, come back. Let me wash at least one piece of your clothing, come back. Let me cup your breasts, come back. Let me drink that teardrop that falls from the corner of your eye after I have made love to you, come back. Let us go to Marine Drive, where you blush when that eunuch calls you 'Kareena', come back. Let me wipe away all your sadness, even if I have to become a clown, come back. Let me say silly things to you. Let me imitate Tom Alter when he speaks Hindi like a rogue British officer in films, come back. Let me teach you to say, 'Nainon,' and kiss your eyes when you get it right, come back. Let me take you to my land and make a snowman, who will have a first-hand physique, come back.*

*

There is an Instagram story of a man, who once loved a girl named Jinan. He fought all of Baghdad for her, he said.

In the end, he ran away from love. He escaped death, he said, but died in any case.

Fi al haroob min al maut
Hu maut aa har

Running away from death is also a form of death.

Someday, she will open his Instagram page and see him like this—his face an island of grief, his eyes softened only with her memory.

He ran away from love; her love. It would have killed him—he truly believed it then. He thought by escaping it, he was escaping death.

But he died in any case, didn't he?

Fi al haroob min al maut
Hu maut aa har

She will not come back. He has lost her.

Still the world goes on.

*

PART THREE

NON-GROUND GROUND

He reaches the café around 2 p.m., and the kid is there. He is happy to see her. As he enters, she walks towards him from the other end, carrying a large tray of glasses, and he wonders if she can reach the washing area without letting them fall. She is so tiny, but walks with feistiness. She sees him and smiles, and it is like sunshine on a cold, foggy afternoon.

Later, when the lunch crowd has thinned, Kim appears. He hugs her.

'Let us run away, Kim,' he says.

She laughs, 'Where to?'

'There is a letter by Emily Dickinson to her friend, in which she writes about a boy who runs away from Amherst, and when asked where he was going, he replies, "Vermont or Asia."'

'What you need is a red,' Kim says.

So, the red arrives in glasses meant for coffee. The café does not have a liquor license yet. But this is a little privilege he has earned, to be offered wine in a lidded coffee tumbler. 'Kim, I got something for that kid.'

'Who?'

'That girl with beautiful braids. I don't know her name.'

Two side braids converge into one straight braid that begins from the top of her head. There is no rationale for this, but he has bought her a pair of Onitsuka Tiger shoes. It is a much smaller size than the one he wears himself. He imagines them posing for a Christmas card in identical shoes—father, daughter. If Adaa and he ever had a child, she would have been roughly sixteen, this kid's age.

This is a new, sudden emotion, and it has come from god knows where. But he has to be careful; his attention towards her—the gift he has bought—may be misconstrued. There are all kinds of men lurking around.

When he sees the child, all he is acutely aware of is this—his missed chance to be a father.

He has heard of women getting these pangs, but he's startled to find such desire rising in his body. He doesn't even like children—everyone knows this. They laugh when he has to be around them in a social gathering; they whisper in each other's ears: 'Look, look, the irritation on his face!' They joke that, in planes, he always attracts the noisiest of children. They say, 'Neel will pay extra for an adult-only airline.'

And yet …

'Oh, you mean Rhythm.'

'Rhythm.' He repeats the name after Kim.

'Sure, give it to her!' Kim says.

'No, I want you to give it to her.'

'It's okay, let me call her.'

Before he can stop her, Kim has called out for Rhythm; she is walking towards them. She has a peculiar habit of shifting her weight from one foot to another. He feels an immense love for her, and in his heart, he says: I will take a bullet for you, kid.

He carefully analyzes this feeling. Is this the male equivalent of what women go through when they fail at love, then decide to adopt a child and raise the kid solo?

Rhythm stands in front of him, and for a moment, he is lost. He imagines her putting her hands on her waist, like demanding kids do, and saying, 'What did you get for me!'

He has guessed the shoe size—it's a rough estimate—and starts crossing his fingers that the size fits. This is his first paternal act and he doesn't want to fail. (*'What, you don't know my shoe size? Do you even know what class I am in?'*) Rhythm steals glances at him as Kim opens the box. He can see that she is excited but is trying her best to control it.

The shoes are kept down, and she looks at Kim.

'Try them,' Kim says.

She removes her sneakers and puts one foot in the right shoe and the other one in the left. She ties the laces carefully, and for a moment, he pictures her in a school uniform. (*'No, Papa will drop me!'* Neel imagines her saying this to a mother he cannot visualize.)

'They are perfect,' Kim says.

It's a reflex he cannot control—he bends and touches the tips of the shoes to feel her toes. The shoes are the right size. The perfect size. With the exact desired space between the big toe and the inner line of the footwear. He feels joyful. He has not failed.

'Okay,' he says.

Rhythm smiles. 'Thank you!' (*'Give me a hug … do you want an ice cream?'*) She bends to take them off.

'Keep them on,' he says.

'Okay,' she answers with glee she cannot hide. She puts her old shoes in the box and walks away.

Kim says the girl is happy. 'It is a beautiful day!'

Indeed.

Behind the counter, where she has joined the other waiters, Rhythm shows off her shoes. The staff looks in his direction.

From that moment, Rhythm becomes 'your kid'. Friends know about his bond with her, but they have no idea what he feels.

'Where is your kid?' they ask when they cannot see her.

'Oh, it is Thursday, it is her day off,' he says, as if she were still asleep when he left home, and he had left her a note on the fridge: '*Darling, I made pancakes. They are on the kitchen counter. Don't watch too much TV. Don't forget to shut the fridge door. Want to watch a movie tonight? Love you, Pops.*'

Rhythm has her own demons, and it is a miracle that she is capable of smiling. She spends much of her time on a bunk bed in a children's home. The atmosphere in the café, its liveliness, the Norah Jones playlist, the playful waitresses senior to her, and the realization that fate can be fought—these have done her good. She is learning, she is opening up.

The other day, Kim says, Rhythm had called her out and said that her seniors were having coffee during their breaks, and she should be allowed, too. 'She has grit,' Kim laughs; Kim told her that she could have as much coffee as she wanted.

When he comes to the café, Rhythm's face lights up. Behind the counter, he can see that the others are teasing her. She approaches him, says hello without looking into his eyes, and keeps a glass of water on the table. She refills it as soon as it is emptied. She is a trainee; she cannot take orders, not yet. He sees that she is wearing her Onitsukas; so is he.

'Oh, same to same,' he says, raising his shoe a bit.

She laughs.

She starts following him on Instagram. He hadn't anticipated this; he didn't know that she was on it ... but it is no surprise. Kids these days are fast with technology; he is aware that her seniors are on social media, so they must have set her up. He immediately follows her back. He reads her posts and stories, and realizes how clueless he has been. She is on the cusp of womanhood. She has tried make-up and uses the latest romantic songs from Bollywood films as background music for her reels. She dabbles with filters. She poses with her friends, and she is searching for love—not fatherly love, but one where there will be a kiss, a rose, a teddy bear and heartbreak. She doesn't need ice creams from a parent; he cannot iron her school uniform and send her off.

He could have offered her so many things. He wouldn't have bought her storybooks but would have made storybooks for her. For school, where everyone is obsessed with English, he would have taught her Hindi that bedazzled onlookers. He would have recited to her fantastic ditties, involving Sindbad and Mowgli. And such great poems! She would have never struggled with Dharamvir Bharati's '*Toota Pahiya*'. She would have been aware that Jatayu had a brother called Sampaati. She would have known of quantum entanglement, and in a world filled with names that do not mean anything, she would have a name with history. She'd have had sound general knowledge, and she'd have known who Plato was, and she'd have had a poster of Hannah Arendt in her room, next to whoever the kids revere these days.

*

Tanya messages him. 'You have disappeared; at least tell me that you won't message, because there has been nothing from you.'

'Remember your morphine promise.'

'Ya, ya, but seriously, where the F are you?'

I am here, Tanya. On the back of a stationary horse; and I refuse to find its bridle.

*

Gargi is in Delhi and wants to meet.

She has moved to Singapore. She has come to India to see her mother, who has developed dementia. 'She only asks for me now,' she says.

He cannot make out if she is happy or sad about it. She is lifting weights and is into a more regimented kind of fasting. He asks her to come to Kim's café.

Gargi arrives with a ton of kohl around her eyes. He cannot laugh, it will make her angry.

'Have you turned Goth?'

'I want my eyes to do all the talking,' she says. She asks for a glass of wine. 'I am hungry. I haven't eaten anything since yesterday afternoon.' She goes through the menu. 'Is there anything non-carb I can order?'

He orders lamb chops for her.

'So, tell me what is going on?' she says.

It is futile to tell her about Aarani's marriage and his heartbreak. It is not that she won't empathize, but he cannot use that empathy as a divining rod to find his way to the woman he loves.

The lamb chops arrive, and she takes a few mouthfuls. She washes this down with wine. 'I couldn't live here anymore,' she says, apropos to nothing.

She has found it difficult to make her peace with 'he who cannot be named'—it is a term in vogue among those who like to say such things. It refers to the chief of India's new political order—an order that has made redundant the beneficiaries of the old political order's largesse. Gargi is not part of Lutyens' Delhi, but she still likes to believe that she is on the right side of history.

'It is terrible, what they have done to this country,' she goes on.

'What do you mean?' he asks, even if he knows what she means.

She is surprised that he is asking her this. But she indulges him anyway. 'Look at the polarization, so much hatred, so many divisions,' she says.

'Have you ever eaten an ice cream at India Gate at night?'

She looks at him and her face contorts. She is not sure where this conversation is going.

'Well, several times. You know, when I was a child, my grandfather used to take us in his Fiat—the one that came with a gear near its steering wheel.' She keeps her fork down. 'But why do you ask?'

'I have never eaten an ice cream at India Gate. Not even by day.'

'So? What has that got to do with what I was saying?'

'I cannot leave this country till I have an ice cream at night at India Gate.'

'God. Are you gaslighting me?'

This is one of those terms people her age have come to use too often for everything. It makes them think that they wield power over the narrative, that by saying this they can stay in the middle of things.

He wants to tell her that the wound of polarization has always been there; that those who weren't hurting, sold the fake ointment of the confluence of cultures, through the metaphor of the confluence of two rivers. But the fake ointment could not treat the wound, which also got prodded from various quarters, till it turned gangrenous. Neel wants to tell her that the wound had been prodded long ago in Kashmir; that those who asked the residents to move on (in other words, forget about the throbbing wound) were not interested in what they were going through. In their good houses, they could not feel the ache. Even now, they can't, as terrible things happen, and if they've turned vocal, it's for their own satisfaction—to see themselves as part of the fraternity of resistance.

On Instagram, when he saw people posting reels with that done-to-death Faiz song, it made him laugh.

In the café, Neel offers no resistance. Some things cannot be said over a plate of lamb chops.

After two hours, they prepare to leave. Gargi opens her bag to take out her wallet, but he has already handed over his card to the waiter. As she attempts closing her bag, he sees the corner of a potato chips packet.

He hopes she is healed; he hopes everyone is healed.

*

'So many sacks I transported like that.'

It misses Neel that Rajbir is still speaking to him.

Rajbir owns three taxis that ferry people to airports or hill stations or for pilgrimages. Neel hires him for assignments that can be done by road. For old customers like him, Rajbir makes the exception of driving himself.

In his younger and more reckless days, Rajbir had been hired by a businessman-turned-politician to transport black money from one spot to another. The cash would be filled in sacks. Rajbir told Neel that, sometimes, he'd take out a wad, and it would go undetected; the cash flow was so large that nobody had the time to keep an eye on small deviations. So, he went on pilfering tiny sums—till, one day, the criminals hired by a business rival waylaid him. As he tried to escape, they fired at his vehicle and a bullet grazed his ear. He kept on driving, and the criminals gave up after a few miles of chase. Rajbir was shaken; he could not speak. He quit that day.

Neel knows the story, and Rajbir knows that Neel knows the story. They have left Delhi behind—they've crossed a mountain of garbage, the eateries and a new apartment complex that gives Neel the feeling that it can come down anytime. They also cross the river which is flooded, just like it was the day Neel met Gurnaam for the first time. In an hour, they will reach the point where the hills begin.

Neel's own past is playing in his head, so he zones out. He catches Rajbir's story at its end.

It has not rained since morning, and Neel is thankful for that. Incessant rains have caused the hills to collapse. While driving, Rajbir watches with passiveness video clips of shooting stones flattening out tourist cars. The four-lane highway that leads to Shimla is blocked by landslides. Tourists have stopped coming.

Yet, Neel is going. He needs to be away from the landslides in his heart, and for that, he will have to cross the landslides in mountainous territory.

No one, except Rajbir, can even attempt to reach Shimla at this time. It is dangerous, and Neel does not know if he will make it. But he is willing to take a chance; and he knows that despite the change he has undergone after that near-death experience, Rajbir is willing to take a chance, too.

Neel has left his regular phone behind, taking instead an ordinary phone with him, from which he can only make calls. He has provided this number to Father and his sister.

He plans to stay in Shimla for two months. A flat, rented by a writer friend, has been made available to him. The writer will be gone for two months; she has finally found love and is trying to build new roots elsewhere. The flat belongs to a woman who is a doctor in the government hospital—she lives alone on the floor above his. There has been no water in Shimla for a week. Miraculously, on the day he reaches, supply is restored.

It takes Rajbir over twelve hours to get to Shimla. On the way, not a single vehicle is going towards the hill station. A few are returning, though. It is frightening to see the hills with big patches of deforestation; they have turned bald and brown. Avoiding uprooted trees and rocks that ooze water, Rajbir proceeds with a prayer on his lips; behind him, Neel sits quietly, his Nokia 1510 by his side.

The house is at one end of Shimla, on a narrow road, next to a beauty parlour known quite well in the area. The writer friend had sent him a long voice note a few days ago. 'Put that parlour's location on your GPS. I have asked my help to clean the flat before you arrive. Speak to her and see what arrangement you want with her. Call me if you get stuck with anything. And yes, the parlour woman sells organic eggs as well, if you give her a little notice.'

Rajbir has turned on the GPS on his phone. By the time they stop outside the parlour, it is beginning to get dark. He sees the house to his right. In front of it is a flight of stairs that goes down to a locality. Beyond, there is a valley; and then, some hills. On an orange-coloured bench right outside, a few labourers, wearing their ropes like bandoliers, are taking a short break from ferrying heavy loads. Next to them—a small vegetable shack. Next to that—a man selling roasted corn on the cob.

'When do I come and take you back?' Rajbir asks.

'In exactly two months,' Neel says.

Rajbir nods. He helps him carry one of his suitcases to the second floor. The main door is unlocked, just like the doctor had said. He opens the wooden door, from which resin is oozing out. Rajbir enters behind him and keeps his suitcase near the shoe rack.

'Don't forget you have to return!' Rajbir says.

Neel laughs.

Rajbir laughs too and goes back.

Neel is all by himself now. He unties his shoes and stands at the door, taking in the place. The living room is a rectangle. On one side is a window, opening to the road below. He looks out of it; there is thick mist rising from the lowlands. A deep melancholy grips Neel. He thinks—I have lost my fortitude only twice. Once, when I lost Mother; and then, when I lost Aarani. I will likely meet Mother before I meet Aarani.

There are two shelves of books by the window, and next to these, a writing desk. On the wall behind, there's the previous occupant's writing schedule. He smiles as he goes through it, and then stops reading it midway; it feels like an intrusion of privacy. There are two bedrooms. There is a four-poster bed in one; Neel knows that this means as much to his writer friend as knives mean to him. He takes the other bedroom. Its walls are damp, so he opens the door and windows to let air in. He remembers, at all other times, to keep the windows locked; the friend, in an earlier conversation, had warned him of a horde of monkeys that regularly paid visit and were invested in ransacking the things inside.

He unpacks fast, keeping almost everything in what will be his bedroom now. He takes quick stock of the kitchen and makes note of the things he will need to buy—tea, milk, eggs, bread. He can purchase these tomorrow, he thinks. He lights a cigarette and sits on the chair facing the road. It is evening, and a number of people, mostly women, are returning from work and slowly climbing down the stairs, with umbrellas tucked under their arms.

He goes to bed early but cannot sleep for a long time. The bedroom windows are curtained. But through the drapes, a dance of lights—playing out from the headlights of passing vehicles—reaches him. Around midnight, it begins to rain heavily, and he finally falls asleep, lulled by the sound.

It is drizzling when he wakes up. It is early, and barring a crow by the railing and a dog below, both wet to the bone, there is nobody on the road at this time. There is a little nip in the air, and it makes him shiver. He puts on a hooded sweatshirt, and immediately sets out to do what he has come for. His notebooks, pencils, pens, markers and little cards (on which he makes mind maps) are all neatly laid out on the table. His hands almost twitch. They need the dopamine of the internet. But today, it's absent. Like a child who begins to cry for milk, and then accepts defeat and goes quiet, the twitching stops after some time. He keeps his focus on the notebook in front of him and writes a paragraph. And then another. For the most part, he sits quietly as nothing comes to him. But he knows it will if he resists the temptation to get up and escape. This desk has to be his penitentiary.

After a couple of hours, the sound of daily life comes to him from the outside. He makes coffee, and lights a cigarette, and stands outside in the balcony. The rain has stopped, but the sky is covered with woolly grey clouds. On the street below, working women are climbing up, and a garbage collector in her ill-fitted fluorescent vest is picking up garbage bags mauled by dogs.

In the balcony of the house right across, he sees a woman holding the hand of a girl who walks with a little stoop. The girl is trying to say something, but it comes in the form of short, incomprehensible bursts of air. The woman seems to understand her. She responds by talking back, and it makes the girl chuckle in delight. After some time, they sit on a bench in the balcony. They don't notice him. In the days to come, he learns that this is a daily ritual for the two of them. The girl is not a girl, but a woman, and the older of the two is the mother—this strikes him after a week or so. The daughter has cerebral palsy, and the little walk in the L-shaped balcony is her way of getting exercise. After a few rounds, when mother and daughter sit on the bench, the daughter pushes her palm towards the mother, to which the mother responds by pushing the palm back. It is their little game—the young woman's way of expressing her love for the one who has birthed her.

He walks to Mall Road, using a map he buys from the local bus stand. It is an uphill trek, and he walks slowly, and then, after a while, when his lungs get used to the altitude, he breaks into a slow jog. He crosses the post office, beyond which is a wall with beautiful green moss, and then, a little ahead, a waterfall, which has empty water bottles and packets of wafers thrown into it. There are very few tourists in the market, but local residents pass him by; they amble, and stop, and greet one another. On Mall Road, past the bookshop and the Chinese shoemaker, there is a coffee house. He enters it. A few old-timers sit at tables, and many of them read newspapers, as waiters in shabby uniforms pass through to the kitchen and back. He waits at an empty table, his face to the road. It could rain anytime. He asks a waiter to bring him a coffee. It comes quickly, and he takes two sips and leaves it. He is put off by the layer of cream at the top, the flat taste of the coffee powder, and the fact that the establishment has scrimped on milky hot water. He pays and leaves. On his way back, he stops at the local bakery and buys bread and buns and a packet of coconut cookies. He walks towards the chief minister's residence, and then past the police headquarters. At a bend, from where he has to go downhill towards his residence, he finds a decent grocery store. He picks things up and puts them in a basket. He pays at the counter, and as he is about to gather two shopping bags, the owner looks at him.

'Where do you live?' he asks.

He tells him the name of the parlour.

'Wait … let me send someone with you to carry these bags.'

Neel say no; he doesn't need help, he can carry them. But the owner says that there is a staffer who has to go that way in any case. So, he relents. A young man—he is in his early twenties; his name is Rakesh—emerges from a small room behind the counter. Neel smiles at him, and he smiles back. Rakesh picks up the heavier bag, while Neel picks the lighter one. Neel comes out, and as he turns right, Rakesh stops him. 'We go left,' he says. Neel follows him, and he sees a small road going downhill. On both sides, there are small shacks selling milk and vegetables. 'By this road, we reach in half the time,' Rakesh says.

Rakesh is curious about the outsider's life. Neel tells him that he is going to be around for two months. Rakesh is appearing for his final year exams and works part-time in the shop to earn an income. His father is employed in the defence sector and is trying to find a job there for his son.

'Is this what you want?' Neel asks Rakesh.

Rakesh goes silent for a moment. 'I have friends who went to Delhi for work. But they say there is no life there. It is better to have smaller dreams, and not leave the place where you are born,' he says. Another pause, and then he adds, 'After I get a job, I will marry here only.'

Neel looks at him and smiles as they keep walking downhill.

'So, how did you get to the shop?' Rakesh asks.

Neel tells him that he had walked up Mall Road.

'That is quite a long way. City people don't walk that much usually,' he says in his soft, polite voice.

'I am a runner,' Neel replies, 'although running here means something else. But I will get better in a week or so.'

In ten more minutes, they are outside Neel's flat.

'Oh, you live in Doctor Madam's house,' Rakesh says.

Neel puts some money into his pocket. 'No, no, it is my job,' Rakesh protests. But Neel presses his hand, and he gives up. 'Thank you,' Rakesh says.

As Neel turns, Rakesh adds, 'Sir, give me your number.' And then: 'On weekends, we sometimes walk through the forest, all the way to the Tara Devi Temple. You will love it. Would you like to come next time?'

'I would love to,' Neel says.

They exchange numbers. Rakesh, Neel sees, is looking at his old-school handset. 'This is just to be away from the city that even your friends disliked,' he says. Rakesh nods; Neel is suddenly reminded of his first conversation with Lakshman in that cut-off area.

As he climbs up to his accommodation, he sees a young woman waiting by the stairs outside his flat. This is Tilla, the house help who works at the doctor's house and had managed his friend's place as well. He calls her in. There is not much to do; more so because he does not want to get sucked into the daily management of a household. He asks her to come twice a week for cleaning. And on those days, she can also cook for him, which will last him till her next visit.

'You will manage like that?' Tilla asks, as if this is an extraordinary thing.

'Yes, Tilla, I will.' He gives her money, and she buys vegetables and some homemade cottage cheese from the vendor below. She prepares this, along with dal.

That evening, he runs into the doctor as she walks past his flat to get into hers.

'Hello, Neel.'

He invites her in for coffee. She is in her mid-fifties, with short hair, and, as Neel notices later, always in a sari. Every morning, at nine sharp, she drives her car to the hospital, past Mall Road, and returns at six.

'I hope you can finish your book in peace. Nobody will disturb you here. If you need anything, just call me,' she says.

Later in the evening, she sends a local delicacy through Tilla.

He again wakes up early the next day. The light has not yet appeared fully outside. He gets to the desk and begins work. He looks out, after a spell of immersion in writing, and sees that it has begun to drizzle again. There is a forlornness to it, but somehow, it does not touch him this time. The two women have started their daily walk in the balcony across. The sounds of school vans, and of cars belonging to early office-goers, and of a bus, reach him every few minutes. But these will soon go away, he knows, and then a silence, which is not absolute, but close, will surround him again.

He eats a breakfast of eggs after he has finished writing a couple of pages. When he feels stuck, he pauses and sits on the chair between the desk and the bookshelves. He takes out a book randomly, and reads a passage or two, after which he returns to write.

The rain is unrelenting. It stops occasionally, and only for a brief period. There is a dampness that pervades everything he touches.

Tilla comes twice a week, as planned. After the first week, he doesn't even tell her what to make.

On Sundays, he takes a break. He leaves in the morning and begins a slow run towards Mall Road, past the fire station. His lungs have got used to high altitudes, and he has also kept his smoking in check. He is on a strict ration of two cigarettes a day; he allows himself to smoke only after the assurance that the writing is progressing well. He runs towards the Indian Institute of Advance Study, beyond which is a forest. He keeps running on the narrow trail till he has exhausted himself. And then, he returns, stopping near the Ramakrishna Mission, at a small hotel, where he eats breakfast and consumes multiple cups of tea.

On some days, when the sun comes out, he takes a ride in the doctor's car till the point where vehicles are allowed.

From there, he walks to Mall Road. He sits in a café and works till lunchtime. The café is staffed by young girls from Spiti, who are in Shimla to study. Supervising them is a wolf-like manager; Neel dislikes him the moment he sets foot into the café. After he enters, he takes a table as far away as possible from the manager. On his way out, he replenishes his stock of buns and takes the shortcut that Rakesh had showed him to his flat.

'I googled you after I was told you'd come,' the doctor says one day, as he rides with her.

'So, what did you find?' he asks.

'You have been to some really terrible places,' she says. Her mobile phone rings. Usually she takes it; Neel knows that she gets a lot of calls from her patients. But this time, she does not answer. 'You go to these places, ferret out journalistic pieces. Maybe some things change after you file your story. But how does the story change you?'

'I was once in a remote area, and came across this really old woman who lived alone; one by one, her family members died. She was incapable of walking six miles to the nearest source of water, a well that had almost dried up. One day, a volunteer from an NGO brought her a blue plastic drum and filled it with water. She couldn't believe it. Her back bent, she asked the volunteer if he could also give her something to eat. She kept smiling while she said this, because she did not want to look ungrateful. I cannot forget that woman's face.'

He does not tell the doctor, but he is missing Mother. She had so much resilience at one time. She could walk up and down hills that housed Himalayan pit vipers and bears, to implement immunization programmes. And then, a helplessness—different from the one carried by the old woman who hoped for food and water—took over, for which no febrifuge was available.

How does the memory of a person end?

To whom does one tell the things one remembers?

'Have a good day,' the doctor says as she drops him at the usual point.

'You, too, Doctor.'

Late in the afternoon, as he is returning, he gets a call. It is from Rakesh. 'Sir, a couple of friends and I are going to Tara Devi through that forest trail tomorrow. Do you want to come?'

The next day is a Saturday. He has to work. But he can take a holiday and work on Sunday.

'I will come, Rakesh.'

The next morning, at 7 a.m., as he climbs up to the grocery store, Rakesh and three others are waiting for him. One of them wears a cap and is carrying a stick in his hands. 'This is for fending off monkeys. Sometimes, in the forest, they like to harass you,' Rakesh says.

They start walking down. At one point, they branch out into a narrow road—it had once been built of concrete, but is now falling apart. After five minutes or so, the road comes to an end; they keep walking downhill along a slippery trail. Thirty minutes later, they are inside a forest of oak and pine and deodar trees. Rakesh talks to his friends, sometimes in Himachali, but for the most part they walk quietly.

Memories of Gurupriya run through Neel's body.

Once, at camp, he found her humming a line from a Telugu song. She was sitting by herself, drawing something on the ground with a little stick. She was so immersed in the act that she didn't notice him. Suddenly, when he drew close, she grew alert.

'No class enemy; it is me,' he said.

'What if you become one tomorrow?'

'What if I do?'

'Then M will shoot you.' She laughed.

'You won't?'

She looked at him, then fixed her eyes on the ground. 'Maybe not,' she mumbled.

Now, he tries to remember that song, but he cannot. He remembers a word, 'prem', from it, but nothing else. The tune does not come to him. He keeps mumbling 'prem' on loop, hoping that the song will follow. But it evades him.

'Sir, you said something?' Rakesh asks.

'No, I was just trying to remember ... it's nothing.'

At some point—by now he has lost all sense of time and does not want to look at his Garmin—they start climbing the other side of the forest; they eventually reach the Tara Devi Temple. Here, he breaks away from the group for a little while, preferring to be by himself. He sits in one corner inside the temple and tries to empty his mind of all images.

Rakesh and his friends are waiting for him at the shoe counter.

'I hope I didn't take too much time,' Neel says.

'We are in no hurry,' replies the man with the cap.

On their way back, Neel can hear the monkeys, but the trekkers have been spared any kind of nuisance.

'We are taking a little detour here. You aren't tired, are you?'

'Not at all.'

'Actually, there is a little stream ahead. We can rest there for a while,' Rakesh says.

Neel keeps walking behind them. After fifteen minutes or so, he can hear the stream. They pass through a row of trees, around which shrubs grow. The rain has washed everything, so wherever he looks, the brightness of green stuns. Tiny wildflowers grow near patches of grass. There is a clearing by the stream; it is wet but not muddy. He sees a rock by a tree and lowers himself on it. The four friends sit nearby on the grass. The one with the cap opens his small backpack and takes out a brown-black substance from it. It's hash. He breaks it into smaller fragments, mixes it with a little tobacco, and pushes it into readymade rolling paper. He lights it, looks at Neel, and offers it to him. Neel takes it in his hand and is surprised at himself for accepting it. He has never tried anything beyond cigarettes and alcohol. But today is today, and in the wilderness of the forest he can taste the desolation of his heart. He takes a puff, and the smoke hits his chest; he coughs. Then he takes a deep breath, takes another puff, and another. He passes it.

He stands and feels the trunk of the tree against his back. There is a consciousness that rises inside him, and every thought, every vision that comes to him, comes in a beautiful, distilled form. He slips himself down on the wet grass. The crow that he had heard cawing when he had hidden in the rose bed appears in front of him. Every sound around him has disintegrated, and each note comes to him, does a little trapeze act, and then passes on to make way for another note. The eunuch is saying 'Kareena', and Aarani's laughter washes over him. Gurupriya has emerged out of the bathroom with a towel around her hair. He is outside, on the bed, half lying, fiddling with the worn-out strap of her wristwatch. He is waiting for her. He hears her humming a few lines like she had, many years ago, in the forest.

And now it occurs to him.

Kammani prem …

She walks towards the bed and looks at him.

'You sing well …' he says.

'*Neeku picci patinda*,' she replies. In that forest, lying on that wet, grassy patch, her voice comes so clearly that he assigns a colour to it—amber.

In Telugu, what she had said was: are you mad …

'I am mad. But so are you. What was that song you were humming?'

'It is from this movie my friend took me to see once. It's about how a madman …' She pauses, laughs, then continues, 'A madman like you falls in love with a woman he thinks is an avatar of a goddess, an angel.'

'Sing it again.'

'No.'

'Please.'

She looks at him, feigns anger, and hums it.

Suddenly, she disappears, and in the next vision, she is in DK, in her uniform, her fist raised in that revolutionary greeting. He is on a bike, and after a very bumpy ride, he enters a military camp in the deepest corner of the guerrilla zone, in a place called Jagargunda. In a small hut in this camp, he finds a soldier lying on a wooden bench, delirious with malaria. The soldier gets up, then lies down, gets up, then lies down again, gets up, then lies down. As he gets up once more, his eyes fall on Neel—god knows what he is seeing. The soldier smiles and shouts, '*Kuch laana to nahi hai*?'

How does one explain the meaning of that question—a question that forms the beating heart of love, of family, of home? *Kuch laana to nahi hai*? Is there something that needs to be procured? Is this what the ancient hunter asked when he went out with his club to provide food to his family? Is this what obsessed him when he risked his life, and didn't hesitate to kill another living being?

Neel suddenly becomes that soldier, and in the delirium within a delirium, he sees Gurupriya enter with an AK-47.

He asks: *Kuch laana to nahi hai*?

She says: Take me to the movies.

He asks: Will you kill me?

She smiles and says: Maybe.

Suddenly, someone says: *Keep your mind in hell and despair not*.

He turns back to see Gillian Rose smiling at him. She has an aura around her, as if she has been beatified.

'What you need is Sister Edna,' she says.

'I know her,' he says.

'You do?'

'I know you met her in Oxford in January 1992. She is a nun and a scholar whose ambition, you say, is to identify the intellectual and spiritual reasons why the modern world cannot hear the mysteries of the soul.'

'So you have read *Paradiso*.'

'I know that sometime after meeting Sister Edna, you were diagnosed with cancer. One day, in a train in London, nausea rose inside you. In desperation, you started chanting Sister Edna's name as a prayer.'

'Yes. Now you need to do it,' she says.

As he prays, he sees Adaa coming out of a hospital; she has had a miscarriage. There is nothing to be done; the doctor says such things happen. 'You guys should keep trying,' the doctor suggests, as she writes out a prescription. Neel sees himself mourning the loss of the child—this baby whose hair he had hoped to one day braid (using a vacuum cleaner, like a video, popular on Instagram, had recommended). He already has a name for her, which is the ancient name of the Chenab. He had hoped to buy her Crocs (the abomination can only be neutralized with the innocence and playfulness of a child). She was meant to have an abacus (he had had one when he was three; then an adult stepped on it, and it broke into two). She was supposed to love lemonade (he had pictured her drinking gallons of it) and know how to swim. She was meant to go to a school where there was no homework. She'd be without fear. If someone attacked her home and forced her family into exile, she'd refuse to take it lying down. He had planned to ask her again and again if the place she inhabited felt like home, and if it didn't, he'd keep changing things, till she said, 'Papa, this is it. Home.'

*

When he comes out of his trance, he sees Rakesh sitting by the stream, eating an apple. Two of his friends are sleeping, while the man who offered him the joint is playing a flute. The flautist sees Neel get up and stops. Rakesh turns towards him.

'How was it?' Rakesh asks.

'Was I saying something?' Neel replies.

'Not much. Except ... well ... you were mumbling some South Indian type of song. And saying that you were missing your sister.'

*

At night, he dreams of his house being on a hillock at the edge of a canal. He can see flowerbeds. But to reach the house, to enter it, he must walk over a row of haphazardly kept green and turquoise blue glass bottles. He sees a lover—faceless—who balances herself on the bottles with so much ease that he has the desire to kiss her feet once she steps across.

But how will he enter the house? He cannot see himself balancing his weight on the bottles.

He wakes up; the pain in his abdomen is pronounced, as if he has used his belly to slither over the bottles.

*

There is a distance that appears between him and the world. It is as if somebody has closed the door to it; and the noise it generates has turned into a faint background hum.

He is unaware of what is happening outside. There is no phone, no TV, no newspaper. His only window to the world is the window in front of his desk, and there, the view, even as it shifts, remains the same. Like clockwork, the two women appear for a walk in the balcony, after which they play their little game. The working women leave for work; the dogs rummage through the garbage bags; later, the labourers appear with their tobacco pouches and cheap mobile phones that play Hindi film songs from the '90s. The doctor leaves for her hospital; Tilla comes, cleans, cooks and leaves. Neel stays in the house, writing at the desk, taking a break to read over coffee; twice a week, he goes to the café in Mall Road. Every second day, he calls Father. Are you okay, did you eat, are you taking care of yourself, he asks; Father sometimes offers a little update about the extended family. The call lasts a few minutes. After that, Neel does not speak to anyone throughout the day. The doctor leaves him alone; she already has experience with writers and their desire for solitude. Moreover, her responsibilities in the hospital keep her busy. Neel's interactions with her remain limited to that short car ride—during which she mostly asks about his writing, and he asks her about Shimla. Sometimes, through Tilla, she sends him food, or apples and pears from her family orchard.

It rains almost every day. Now and then, the skies open up with such fury that it seems like everything will be washed away. He looks wearily at the eroded hills and at the houses built haphazardly over them; he feels they can come toppling down any time. The doctor tells him about the destruction she has witnessed. One night, a few houses collapsed as the ground beneath them slipped away; the debris came crashing down to the road below. Some people died, including a former colleague. The bulldozers arrived, they cleared the debris, and life went on.

A handful of tourists still keep coming—out of what compulsion, nobody knows; they buy faux branded clothes on Mall Road, eat momos, and make Instagram reels. As

Neel runs on the elevated road by the old hotel, they gawk at him, startled by the speed at which he thrusts his body forward and the bulge of his calves. They cannot see that the pain in his abdomen radiates all over; or that some images come to him as he sprints, and that he pushes them away, and afterwards, he sits on a ledge, staring into the valley below. At some point, he gets up and begins the long walk back to the house.

He accompanies Rakesh and his friends on a trek once more, but this time he declines to partake of the joint.

One day, the sun comes out, and he puts clothes in the washer and hangs them out to dry. Across the street, the woman (who walks with her mother) is there, and he finds her looking at him. He waves at her and smiles. She smiles too and waves back at him. From then on, it becomes a ritual of sorts. He comes to the balcony and waves at her and she reciprocates. Sometimes, from his desk, he finds her looking towards his balcony in anticipation. He comes out quickly and waves.

Once, he wakes up and finds a huge monkey holding on to the railing of the balcony, sitting in contemplation. As he moves closer, the monkey looks at him. Then it returns to its meditative posture.

Neel studies the calendar and sees that seven weeks have passed. A week later, when the monkey comes, there will be nobody on this side of the window to observe him. The woman across will wonder where he has gone. She will feel a momentary sadness; then, perhaps, she will move on to other things that occupy her mind.

He sits on the chair by the desk and takes in the room, so he can remember it later, at a time when he is no longer here. He closes his eyes and tries capturing the sounds coming from the street below and beyond.

It's unlikely that he will ever be here again. This is the impermanence the world holds; he cannot come to terms with it.

Yet, isn't such impermanence the defining quality of his life; isn't this the paed raah that Father complained about?

The rains become more intense, and then they stop. He cannot bring himself to write; he cannot read. A sudden hunger gnaws at him, and he begins to eat five or six times a day. The food Tilla cooks and leaves for him proves inadequate. He gets bagfuls of cookies and buns and cream rolls and wafers and patties, and consumes them one by one, until he begins to worry that something Mephistophelian has started growing inside him.

On the fifty-ninth day, Rajbir calls. 'Are you ready?' Then he goes on, 'I don't know how I will come, but I will try. There are landslides along the entire highway. Be prepared for a long, arduous journey.'

'Arduous journeys are my fate, Rajbir.'

He laughs. Tomorrow then.

Tomorrow.

*

The next day, he does not look at the balcony across the street. To the doctor he had said goodbye the previous evening.

As he waits for Rajbir, he finds himself thinking of the doctor. Had she been in Delhi, she'd have been living with a cat. But here she is, in Shimla, alone, braving the elements, driving up and down treacherous hills to see patients, wearing her short hair like a pistol. He imagines the loneliness must become stark. Once, at night, when a drunk man crashed his car against a tree near her house, it scared her. Surely, at such times, one desires a pair of arms to keep one secure? The next morning, a cup of coffee must have been the doctor's only comfort.

At last, Rajbir arrives—this, after struggling with shooting stones and fallen trees. The doctor has left for the hospital. Neel has paid Tilla and given her extra money to buy a bicycle for her child. It's time to leave.

Many impediments and detours later, Rajbir and Neel are in the plains. Neel dozes off for a while in the backseat. When he wakes up, he hears Rajbir's voice. He's still sleepy; his voice seems to come from faraway, like a drawl.

'So many sacks I transported like that.'

*

He is back in Delhi—it has been a day—when his phone rings. It's a journalist from Punjab he has known for a long time. Gurnaam is dead; he was found hanging in his house by a neighbour. When Neel hears this, he remembers what Gurnaam had told him over their last meeting—'Then I will go.' Neel had thought that he meant to go to DK; but Gurnaam had been conveying something quite else to him.

An hour later, he is at the airport; around four hours later, he stands with a small group of people in the courtyard of Gurnaam's house. He lies on a cot, draped in a red flag. There have been murmurs that Gurnaam had had major disagreements with his comrades. As things became hot in DK, the rebels had become paranoid; they had recklessly started killing Adivasis on suspicion of being police informants. Was Gurnaam's decision to end his life a political statement? Or was it a philosophical one—because he knew he was becoming old and would soon be dependent on others?

Gurnaam was Neel's friend, and, in a way, his teacher; he was someone who had turned his life in a particular direction.

As fists rise in farewell, Neel raises his and prays for his friend's salvation.

Comrade, may you be free of peedh. May you find a place of rest, a home.

*

An association of almost thirty years with Gurnaam has come to an end. Neel ruminates over the fate of men. There was so much Gurnaam had seen and felt; he had spent time in every corner of DK. What can be said about such a life?

He thinks of his first meeting with the man beside that little memorial. In the short flight back to Delhi, he feels an immense loneliness wash over him.

At home, Father has acquired a smartphone on which he watches random video clips. On WhatsApp, a few relatives send him political videos, but he discards them immediately.

These are what keep conversations going among those in parks and laughter clubs—it disgusts him.

Neel wonders—are these the videos that make the lives of retired men interesting; that make them appear knowledgeable, as though they have worked in a secret society and are aware of things that nobody else does? In truth, the videos boil down to laughable things—like how Nehru had, unbeknownst to them all, embraced Islam.

Father rejects this, and for the first time, Neel is thankful that he is not part of a 'club'. Father sees clips of children singing in a competition, or of a boy performing Dabke in a Palestinian wedding. He is amazed at the boy's sense of rhythm, the dexterity of his limbs.

Sometimes, Neel finds Father seated, thinking. Neel likes to believe that he is thinking of Mother, his wife.

He imagines having a drink with Father and discussing their individual heartaches. But Father does not have in his possession idioms that speak of the heart; and, come to think of it, neither does he.

Neel cannot lay a brick road between himself and Father; there will be no communing.

*

That summer, Neel's sister insists that Father spend a few days at her place. Father has never done it before. He tries offering her a litany of excuses, but this time she does not relent. He looks at Neel, but even he is not coming to his rescue. This cycle of burdensome loyalty must break at least once. Neel cannot leave Father because he thinks his parent cannot function without him; Father did not go anywhere because Mother could die, and now that she is gone, he feels a weary sense of responsibility towards Neel.

It's strange to see him packing the old way, using a cloth bag and a big plastic bag. He does not understand suitcases or duffle bags. 'Eat those apples, otherwise they will rot,' he tells Neel. 'Do not forget to switch off the gas supply at night.' 'Check all windows before you leave for work.' 'Eat on time.' Neel smiles. Neel's sister pulls Father along, and he walks down the stairs and sits in the car reluctantly.

Neel comes back and stands at the door of Father's house. He has a vision of crossing over, of being mauled by a passenger tram and meeting his end. He shrugs this image off and sits on the sofa; he plays some music. From the window, he watches children run after each other in the lawn below. He eats early and goes off to sleep.

He hears something ring. At first, he thinks it is part of his daily phantasmagoria of horror—his commune with the ghouls. But a moment later, he realizes that his phone is ringing. He is startled. He looks at the phone and sees it is an unknown number.

'Hello,' he says.

From the other end, someone says hello. Then, he adds: I have some samachar to offer.

It suddenly comes to Neel—it's Lakshman.

'Lakshman, is it you?'

'Yes, it is me. Remember me?'

'Of course. Are you okay?'

'I am okay. There has been a big operation in the jungle where I took you the last time. Lots of big brothers are dead,' he says.

It began after midnight. There was a lot of gunfire. From a distance, one could see a raging fire.

'Will you come?'

'I am tired, Lakshman.'

'We are all tired,' he says. Then, after a pause, he adds: 'I remember you a lot.'

'I will come and see you again, I promise.'

*

The commandos had been dropped into the jungle. From there, they walked in the night using their GPS sets. The information provided to them of the big camp in the forest came from a source. They surrounded the camp, and right after midnight, as Lakshman had tried explaining, they let loose a rain of rockets. The guerrillas were taken by complete surprise. Some of them tried to escape but were killed by commandos who had positioned themselves along the outer periphery.

*

'It was a big encounter,' the district police chief says in response to Neel's message. It's 8 a.m., two hours after Neel texted him.

'Are there pictures?' Neel asks.

At 9.30 a.m., he receives twenty photos. Against the red loamy earth, the corpses have been laid on black tarpaulin sheets. A masked man collects blood samples from them. Small plastic sample bottles lie next to him. Over the bodies, the commandos—with their guns and jackets and night-vision devices—stand in small groups; a few of them are noting down the details in a long register.

In the eighth photograph, he sees her. Her camouflage shirt has shifted a little, and below it, her intestines are visible. He looks at her hand and a lump of sorrow forms in his throat. He looks at her legs; one of the shoes has come off and her old socks with loose elastic are visible.

Her eyes are open—as though, if he happened to come near her, she'd say, *Neeku picci patinda*.

*

Rohini and Gunaa take refuge in a cave. He is a mad man but—to put it in Deleuze's words—she is about to grasp the kernel of madness in him, and that will make her fall in love with him; he, in turn, will love her to a point where every point becomes pointless.

He says he wants to write her a letter. But as he cannot, he wants her to write it.

Read it out to me, and then you can read it for yourself, he says.

In the cave, Rohini's voice echoes like that of Gurupriya. 'I like it,' she says.

That love letter becomes the song. *Kammani*.

Gunaa says: When I think about you, poems come flooding to my heart.

Neel says: I can only smell coconut oil. Have I lost you?

Gurupriya says: Maybe.

*

In the autumn of that year, nursing his abdominal pain, he gets down from a bus in the small town where he hopes to see M.

M had surrendered after her sister's death. As part of her surrender deal, she had been released a week earlier. She now works as a teacher in a school started by a former lawyer, who had been shot dead by the police for helping activists labelled as Maoists.

She lives near the school in a room with an asbestos roof. Outside, the walls are painted with cheap blue distemper, the sort used to paint tree trunks in parks. She is surprised to see him there—he had not told her that he will be coming.

She smiles, and he hugs her the way he had seen Gurupriya hugging her—with the foreheads touching. As he sits on a stool, she brings him a glass of water from an earthen pitcher. He looks around. The walls inside are also painted with the same distemper. There is a bed and next to it, there are a few books on a rusty table. It is hot. The fan works, but barely.

'Well, this is home now,' she says, smiling.

She goes to make tea. He looks again at the table and finds copies of his books there.

He goes to where M stands; he holds her hand. 'I am sorry about Gurupriya,' he says.

She doesn't look at him; she adds a little milk to the tea.

They talk through the night, just like they had many years ago next to that angry river in DK. At some point, he gets up to make food; he wants her to rest. She looks weak and tired. He goes out, buys some country chicken, and he makes this into a curry. With rice, they consume it, sitting on a mat, eating with their hands.

M speaks about Shailaja. She is responding to treatment; her law practice is going well.

They sleep for an hour or so in the wee hours of the morning. He walks with her to her school; children greet her on the way, and she responds. M and Neel stand at the school gate.

She touches his elbow. 'Do you remember, when we first met, you had asked me why the Adivasi women you saw sat on their haunches on the road? You were worried they'd get crushed by a vehicle ...'

'Yes.'

'They sat that way because the tar road did not impinge on their idea of home. For them, the spot where they sat was still the forest they had known since they were born. It was home.'

It is time to enter the school.

'Goodbye, saathi,' M says.

Then, she adds, 'Find a home.'

She opens her bag and puts something in his palm. It is the Swiss knife he had given Gurupriya. It had fallen from her trousers as the state forces attacked the camp; a guerrilla, who managed to escape from there, picked it up.

'The guerrilla was Jassi,' M says.

*

He finishes writing the book. As he holds the manuscript in his hands, he catches sight of his reflection on the windowpane, beyond which is the city where, the newspaper reports tell him, twenty thousand marriages are taking place that night. The sorrow nerve, which Aarani had noticed, beats like a heart. Around it, his face is beginning to look more and more like Father's, except for the thin upper lip, which is a memento from Mother.

He remembers that he has something in his drawer—a blurred photo of Aarani, printed on matte paper, taken one Sunday in the Mumbai hotel. In it, she is in bed, a white quilt over her legs, her arms behind her head, an elbow concealing her face. She looks like a Renaissance painting. Here, she belongs to him. Here, she will always belong to him. When he is dying, he knows this image will pass before his eyes like a film. Nobody can take it away from him.

He takes another look at the picture, and he whispers what Heidegger had told Hannah Arendt in a letter. *Amo: Volo ut sis.* I love and I want you to be.

He is home; he must stop looking for ground. He must build it himself. And he must build it here. He must keep his grief private, and now, he must drop anchor.

He must stop thinking of Dachau when he comes across exposed brickwork.

He walks out to the living room and sees Father tending to a plant that has lost its Rausch.

'Have you eaten?' Father asks.

'No, I haven't. I will eat soon.'

He returns to his bedroom, reminding himself that he has to go and see Lakshman. He opens a closet and takes out a carton labelled Base Camp. He begins taking things out of it, one by one.

A line from a Nida Fazli nazm comes to him:

Apna gam leke kahin aur na jaaya jaaye;
Ghar mein bikhri hui cheezon ko sajaaya jaaye.

Let's not go anywhere with our sorrow, he tells himself. Let's rearrange the things at home.

ACKNOWLEDGEMENTS

My foremost gratitude goes to Manu Joseph and Sumana Roy, for being the first readers of the novel, and for writing generous endorsements. After looking through the first draft, Manu's belief in what I had set out to do (and what little detours I could take) kept me steadfast on my journey.

Thanks also to Anita Nair, for her friendship, and for her friendship as a novelist, and for knowing which among these to dole out when. To Aruni Kashyap, for lighting small lamps while I was struggling with writing and other vagaries of life.

At HarperCollins, to my editor, Dharini Bhaskar, for seeing things I could not see, or pretended not to see, and for being a co-traveller in this journey; and to Udayan Mitra for his trust in my work.

To my literary agent and friend, Hemali Sodhi, and to Ambar Sahil Chatterjee.

To Uday Foundation's Rahul Verma—brother, friend, grand strategist of life-galaxies—for things that no mathematics can put together.

To Ritu Vaishnav, for her unconditional and deepest friendship, which in today's world is a miracle.

To S. Prasannarajan, for his grace in the uncouth world of Indian journalism.

To Priyanka Dubey, for a little sanctuary in the June of 2023, and to Ruchi Ramesh.

To Bhaskar Bhatt, friend and possessor of old-world goodness of heart.

To Satyen Bhan, friend and enabler of countless things.

To Marci Shore and Stathis Kalyvas, for the luminosity of their scholarship.

To Comrade S., whom I first met decades ago in a small room in north Delhi; and to T., whose stoicism felt like a gold plate over her heartbreak.

To my father, Pran Nath Pandita, for instilling in me a certain fierceness for home.

To Urvashi Pratap Singh, for the base camp of the heart.

And, finally, to Dandakaranya—may it stay away from the illusion of the golden deer.

NOTES

1. The information about David Wojnarowicz's archives is taken from an essay 'The Magic Box' by Olivia Laing, *Granta 126*.

2. The video of the man from Baghdad is from film director Mohannad Abu Rizk's Instagram account.

ABOUT THE AUTHOR

Rahul Pandita is a journalist who is known for his reporting from war-torn areas. He is the author of *Hello, Bastar: The Untold Story of India's Maoist Movement*; *Our Moon Has Blood Clots: A Memoir of a Lost Home in Kashmir*; *The Lover Boy of Bahawalpur: How the Pulwama Case Was Cracked*; and is the co-author of *The Absent State: Insurgency as an Excuse for Misgovernance*. He received the International Red Cross Award for conflict reporting in 2010. He is a Yale World Fellow and also the recipient of the New India Foundation Fellowship. He lives in Delhi.

HarperCollins *Publishers* India

At HarperCollins India, we believe in telling the best stories and finding the widest readership for our books in every format possible. We started publishing in 1992; a great deal has changed since then, but what has remained constant is the passion with which our authors write their books, the love with which readers receive them, and the sheer joy and excitement that we as publishers feel in being a part of the publishing process.

Over the years, we've had the pleasure of publishing some of the finest writing from the subcontinent and around the world, including several award-winning titles and some of the biggest bestsellers in India's publishing history. But nothing has meant more to us than the fact that millions of people have read the books we published, and that somewhere, a book of ours might have made a difference.

As we look to the future, we go back to that one word—a word which has been a driving force for us all these years.

Read.

Harper Collins · 4th · HARPER FICTION · HARPER NON-FICTION · HARPER BUSINESS · HCCB HARPERCOLLINS CHILDREN'S BOOKS

HARPER DESIGN · Harper Sport · HARPER PERENNIAL · HARPER VANTAGE · हार्पर हिन्दी · BOOKTOPUS